A.C. STARK

Ernest & Noble

1st Edition.

Independently Published by A.C. Stark in 2019
Kindle Direct Publishing
email: scribblerstark@gmail.com
www.acstark.net

ISBN: 9781705585191

Author's Note

The characters within this text were first conceived whilst I was exploring and assessing the state of my psychology and philosophical reality. This exploration was, in many respects, both the cause of and caused by my very own existential crisis – an experience which greatly influenced my writing of *Ernest & Noble*.

Indeed, its joint protagonists represented two incompatible parts of my psyche which were waged in a seditious guerrilla war for many years. Between the ages of 20 and 27, whilst reading Philosophy at King's College London and subsequently attempting to establish an ambition-filled, high-tempo London life (the kind of which, unfortunately, is so highly valued and heedlessly sought after in our modern times), I experienced long-lasting spells of dissociation, regular panic attacks, vivid night terrors and sleep paralysis. With neither side ceding ground, it was not until I enquired directly with them both, through writing, that my symptoms of depression slowly dissipated. That war in my head eventually culminated with *Ernest & Noble* and the philosophical conclusions and spiritual revelations discovered within it.

In this sense, this short book serves not only as a philosophical testimony, but as a eulogy to a former self. Ultimately, it was only through *earnest* that a solution to my own existential crisis was (possibly) found.

A.C. Stark

Thanks

Without the encouragement, curiosity, suggestions and support received from many friends and relatives of mine this text would not exist in its current form. As my first printed publication, the journey that *Ernest & Noble* took me on was immensely intellectually stimulating, often depressing but, eventually, rather liberating. I therefore wish to extend my thanks to Olyver Cox and Olivia Loveridge for their feedback on the early drafts; to Josh Grear and Henry Braime respectively for the time we shared discussing and musing over the many topics touched upon in the book; and to Jenefer Stark, my wonderful wife, for being my personal sounding board, which is never an easy task.

For the vestiges of humanity.

Ernest & Noble

CONTENTS

Part One: An Atheist's Theodicy   **10**

Chapter 1
A Cause for Concern   11

Chapter 2
The Philosophical Atheist   27

Chapter 3
Ethical Instrumentalism   39

Chapter 4
The Pernicious Paradox   48

Chapter 5
The Importance of Meaning   61

Chapter 6
Nietzsche, Nihilism and the Nazis   70

Part Two: Searching for Salvation   **86**

Chapter 7
Prudentialism   88

Chapter 8
Giving Credence to the Conscience   105

Epilogue
Afterwards   121

Part One
An Atheist's Theodicy

As always, we begin nowhere near the beginning. For that, we would have to trace back through millennia, to a time well before the surveillance, digital and industrial ages, prior to the Enlightenment, back to when things had meaning. Instead, we begin towards the end, in an ancient setting, in a contemporary, cosmopolitan city. Fleet Street, London. Halfway between the bronze chiming bells of St. Paul's Cathedral and the Georgian-cum-utilitarian-cum-faux-Victorian architecture constituting Somerset House and the Strand Campus of King's College London. We begin in a timeworn public house. A pub riddled with knots, knobs, warts and crannies. A tavern as creaky and withered as a dogged war veteran plagued with rheumatoid arthritis; which smells like the smouldering remnants of damp ashwood and stale hops. We begin in the same place as we shall end, in an alehouse once frequented by the likes of Charles Dickens; these days an eclectic hub, brimly filled with hipsters, yuppies, wayfarers and academics: Ye Olde Cheshire Cheese Inn. Here, by the fire. This is where the discussion took place - a deep, dark and doomful discussion, a *philosophical* discussion - between the very earnest Ernest and the notably most noble Noble.

But first, a warning: I implore you, please, do not delve into this text unwittingly. And for the sake of your sanity, if you do enter the labyrinth here within these pages, do not give up it until you have read it in its entirety. For, if you do, you will likely return from it torn and scarred, enfeebled, *different*. Especially, that is, if you are an atheist.

Chapter 1
A Cause for Concern

Earnest: Having or displaying a deep and sincere conviction; ardent.
Adjective *"an earnest student"*

Ernest, a spirited, headstrong and somewhat haughty second-year undergraduate, having been ejected the previous evening from the Strand Campus bible study group, heedlessly divulges his contention that God is not as assuredly good as Christians have traditionally been led to believe. With a hoarse voice and ceaseless determination, he battles to have his *logic* heard and - more importantly - appreciated.

Noble: An elevated moral or psychological character; magnanimous.
Adjective *"a noble sentiment"*
Noun A noble man or lady; person of high ranking; a nobleman.

Entertaining him is his new friend and seminar leader, Noble, whose personal endeavour towards securing a Doctorate of Philosophy has long since stagnated on account of him unwittingly wading from one existential crisis to the next. He sits with rosy, wine-pinched cheeks and a dispassionate glazed expression. With his jaw resting in the palm of his hand and the appearance of a well-fed urban racoon, he becomes increasingly concerned with Ernest's pugnacity and begins to contemplate doing something about it.

Ernest
To sin, and salvation!

Noble
... and sedition.

Ernest
Oh, come on. That's hardly fair.

Noble

Then tell me what actually happened.

Ernest

I simply told Father Chance that Jesus obviously had the power to show everyone God's will, but he only showed it to the few that he favoured. St. Paul for instance.

Nothing too controversial, as I think you'd agree.

Noble

Yes. But what did you say after that?

Ernest

Well. I said that it follows that Jesus must have repressed his followers.

Noble

Ah! I see. I don't expect he agreed with your opinion there?

Ernest

Yeah. Well, no he didn't. And it isn't really *my* opinion - I don't believe any of it. It just follows from logic: that *if* Jesus's story is true *then* he must have repressed his followers - everyone in fact.

Noble

Perhaps. I think I can see how you might think that, but explain your logic anyway.

Ernest

Fine. Well, Jesus apparently turned water into wine, right? He healed the suffering and calmed the storms. He obviously had miraculous powers. So, he must have had the power to telepathically reveal God's will to *everyone* simultaneously--

Noble

Therefore, since Jesus chose to reveal the will of God to merely a select few, it follows that he must have decided to withhold it from the masses, which would have amounted, in your mind at least, to the repression of humanity?

Ernest

Yeah, pretty much.

Noble

An interesting perspective, Ernest - I'll give you that. No wonder Father Chance was positively plucking at feathers when I saw him last. Yet, how do you account for the freedom of the will? Surely he asked you that.

Ernest

Freewill was mentioned but how is it even relevant?

Noble

The argument goes that moral suffering exists precisely because of freewill. God endowed humanity with freewill and in doing so he enriched the universe; he made it better.

Ernest

Yeah. And?

Noble

And so God is not to blame for the actions of man.

Ernest

Mhm.

Noble

Yes, well, before the beginning, God had the option to create a wholly determined universe, wherein this very conversation - and your unwavering lust for truth - might have been foreordained by the fusion of past events with the perpetual laws of nature. Or, alternatively, God had the option to create a universe comprised in part by freew--

Ernest

Freewill. Yes, yes.

Noble

In the second of those possible universes - in *our* universe - evil actions, and any suffering that consequently follows, occurs because of the existence of freewill. That is, sometimes, through having freewill people choose to do things which cause others harm. This is where the terms moral suffering and moral evil come from. That notwithstanding, this universe remained preferable to God because of the *richness* of freewill.

Ernest

Yeah, *of course*. The basic freewill defence. I've studied Plantinga. I know all this but what is the relevance?-- that Jesus *freely chose* to repress humanity? I agree! That's what I told him.

Noble

Yes, of course, but that is not what I am trying to show you. Perhaps I might better convey my point with a question. Would revealing God's will telepathically to every free, sentient being in every corner of the universe not constitute a betrayal of their freewill, and would that not exhibit a deeper form of repression than that you accuse of Jesus?

Ernest

No. obviously not. They'd still have freewill despite their shared revelation.

Noble

Ah, but would they, *truly*? Perhaps. Yet, perhaps we should remember the purpose of freewill. The purpose of freewill is that people are able to *freely choose* God. If this is true, then it is without question that a communal telepathic revelation would have contravened the entire purpose of freewill; the very reason God endowed humanity with it.

Ernest

This I find bemusing.

Noble

You do?

Ernest

I mean, I get it: if humanity simultaneously received a revelation, as individuals they'd retain their freewill as a mode of action but that *will* would not necessarily remain *free* in the proper sense. It would be, to some degree, hindered because it would from thereon be affected in some way by their revelation. And, however small that affect might be, it would still constitute a sort of impediment on the will, making it less free.

Noble

Good.

Ernest

But the idea that God endowed us with freewill purely because he wanted us to find and worship him is too horrific to bear. I mean, how vain! God is supposed to be benevolent but isn't vanity a deadly sin?!

Noble

It is, Ernest. But--

Ernest

Then why are you, like Father Chance, so unconvinced by this *logic*? There are so many contradictions within religion - *especially* the Abrahamic ones - it's hard to understand why people even entertain it, let alone *believe* in it.

Noble

But--

Ernest

What you have proved for me so far is that Jesus repressed humanity because he didn't want to impede upon their freewill, because doing that would have stopped humanity from being able to *freely choose* God. So, Jesus repressed humanity so that God could indulge himself in his own furtive narcissism.

Noble

Er, yes, I suppose, well, that may well be someone's position. Though, not anyone I know of. But--

Ernest

But God is supposed to be wholly-good! Should he not therefore put the well-being of humanity above his own narcissism - his own need to be the centre of attention, his own need to feel loved? So, the suggestion that a universe with freewill in it is better than one without is flawed: morality should not derive from vanity!

Noble

Ah yes, but, *vanity*?

Ernest

Yes, vanity! He created a freely living human race *in his own image* and then effectively demanded them to love and worship him. That's the deistic equivalent of stroking yourself in the mirror!

Noble

What?! Er. Well. I, I see what you mean.
   I can't say your argument is not a good one, strictly logically speaking.

Ernest

Mhm.

Noble

Though, have you considered ineffability?

Ernest

Yeah. Ineffability is a copout.
   Why are you on Chance's side? Logic is logic.

Noble

Indeed it is, tautologically so. Yet, perhaps Jesus was incapable of communicating God's will to everyone telepathically. He was human after all.

Ernest

Another contradiction! How can something be both God *and* human? Jesus performed miracles, so he was not human; humans cannot perform miracles. Miracles are absolute in their essence; the laws of nature are either broken or they are not. So he wasn't human.

Noble

Is it not conceivable that some miracles may be smaller or greater than others?--

Ernest

Wel--

Noble

And that, as such, perhaps Jesus was incapable of greater miracles; miracles of the magnitude of that you speak - i.e., telepathically transferring his knowledge of God to one and all simultaneously?

Ernest

Well, no. Things are either possible or impossible. There is nothing in between. Neither can anything be more impossible than impossible; there is no such thing as *more*-impossible. Impossible is impossible; nothing more, nothing less.

Accordingly, I think we can justifiably assume that if Jesus had the power to do the impossible, he could have done anything within the realm of impossibilities, including spreading God's word telepathically to *everyone*, rather than just a select few. Yet, he didn't. *Why*? Because he was not the Saviour, but a repressor.

Noble

Ernes--

Ernest

In the Gospels Jesus insists that he was not the source of his own powers, but that God was. So, why would God limit Jesus's powers? *Because God is a corrupt narcissist.*

Another thing. Listen, the book of John clearly states that Jesus and God are one; that they are consubstantial, right?

Noble

Yes.

Ernest

So, Jesus is supposed to be both wholly human and wholly God.
But if God *is* Jesus, then how can he put limitations on himself?
The answer to the age-old question of whether God can create
a stone that God cannot lift is: yes! Yes God can! Which does the
theist's position no good at all, as you well know.

Noble

The concept of a self-limiting God is well written about, Ernest.
Many people do think that Jesus and God are consubstantial
and that God is self-limiting. I will happily detail the arguments
for you.

Ernest

No, please don't. Like I said, I've studied this, I know the
arguments from Olson and Vardy and, erm... William of
Ockham, about the difference between God's 'absolute' and
'ordained' powers.

Noble

Then I would expect you to be more sceptical and less
forthright--

Ernest

Sure. But...
Listen: if I played football with my little nephew, a
toddler, I wouldn't play to my fullest ability, would I? I'd limit my
abilities so that he can enjoy himself, right? My 'ordained power'
would limit me to play on my knees, for instance. But I would
always retain the ability to override this self-limitation and play
to my fullest, most 'absolute power' if I wanted to. Yeah?

Noble

Yes, I understand.

Ernest

Analogously, God can create a stone he cannot lift, provided he
abides by the rules of the game. But the reason he cannot lift it

is not because he is *incapable* of lifting it, but because the rules of the game state that he is *not permitted* to lift it. So, it follows that if Jesus was God, then Jesus was merely playing a game.

What I mean is he imposed rules upon himself which restricted his powers, but he always had the ability to override those rules. So, it follows logically that he chose not to. Jesus, or God, *chose* to repress humanity.

Noble

Erm. Yes, well. In honesty, Ernest, I respect your logic. You pose an extremely controversial argument but a thorough one all the same. I am not at all surprised Father Chance found you challenging.

Ernest

Thank you!

Noble

Yet, I must say, I fail to understand why you attended the bible study in the first place, other than for the purposes of testing Father Chance. Or maybe you went to challenge the faith of the other attendees.

Ernest

Well--

Noble

I fear that you fail to realise the assumptions upon which these arguments of yours are founded.

Ernest

What assumptions?

Noble

You are impassioned, Ernest. You should carry your assumptions. You should not be carried away by them.

Ernest

Okay, sure, but what assumption?

Noble

You seem to have an almost blind trust in logic. You share a sentiment that very many atheists seem to presently hold - that the exposition and acceptance of scientific universal truths constitutes a moral categorical imperative. Which is extremely problematic for several reasons, not least because 'truth' is a slippery thing.

Maybe I'm wrong, I'm not sure. Though I do think that you assume truth, or perhaps rationality to be above all else of utmost importance. Everything that cannot be understood rationally - or scientifically, rather - is meaningless to you.

Ernest

Well it is, isn't it?

Noble

In honesty, I'm uncertain. Though, I don't believe it is. And I wouldn't dare to steadfastly assume it is either. That could be a very dangerous thing indeed.

Ernest

Really? *How*?

Noble

Ernest, there are two things that I can take away from this conversation of ours. The first can be described as a virtue, but the second; the second I fear presents a grave danger and deeply worries me.

Ernest

...

*   *   *

Noble spots a man sitting at the bar thumbing his way through a copy of the Independent and recognises the issue, vividly recalling the soul-shaking image on the front cover. Its main story was about Anders

Breivik, a far-right extremist who shot dead sixty nine members of a summer youth camp on Otoya Island in Norway in 2011. It revealed how, in the immediate aftermath, various online media outlets made the crude assumption that it was an Islamic extremist terror event, rather than what it really was - an islamophobic plot of revenge. Breivik justified his actions on shallow and uneducated ideas; on beliefs that he held, without a drop of scepticism, to be *absolutely* true. Noble had felt sick reading the article; sick from the concern that such an immense level destruction could emanate from such a basic and confused idea.

As the pages are turned again, Noble captures the flicker of another memorable article. It was an article about the mental health crisis reportedly permeating society - a regular theme in the columns these days. He remembered a thought he'd had at the time of his own reading of the paper: Was it all interconnected? Might absolutism, as a newly invigorated normative phenomenon, be partly responsible for society's shared sense of self-denial, as well as for these modern acts of extremism?

Ernest

>Go on...

Noble

>Er. Sorry.
>>The first is that your ability to analyse and synthesise ideas is most impressive. You could perhaps work on how you articulate yourself. Nevertheless, I am confident you will be successful in whatever you do after university.

Ernest

>Well, thank you.

Noble

>You're welcome.
>>The second, however, is that your vehemence, your steadfastness, could one day become extremely damaging to others, perhaps even to yourself. Honestly, you'd benefit greatly if you learned to be just a little more tactful with your words.

Ernest

Yeah, well I don't need to be tactful with you do I?

Noble

I may go so far as to say that-- and please excuse any wrongful assumptions I might make here...

Ernest

Go on.

Noble

You are manifestly an atheist?

Ernest

Yes.

Noble

I might go as far as to say that militaristic atheism-- and again, I am not necessarily accusing you of being militaristic, but militaristic atheism is morally wrong. The danger, as I see it, is that your passion for truth may one day compel you that way.

Ernest

Well, isn't it written in the Bible that Christians should *go forth* and spread the word?

Noble

It is.

Ernest

What about the Jehovah's? Evangelicals? Do some Muslims also not believe that their faith obliges them to promote Islam?

Noble

Indeed. I understand, and I be--

Ernest

So?

Noble

Well, I believe I have an answer. This is what you are saying - correct me if I am wrong. You are saying that people of various faiths believe, through having experienced some kind of revelation, that they have the *truth*. In their eyes, they have experienced spiritual and moral emancipation and are thus morally obligated to share this truth with others, to save them in some sense, to grant them emancipation also.

Ernest

Yeah.

Noble

And this act of delivering the truth is viewed by its messengers, as it were, as being an inherently good act. This is what you mean, correct?

Ernest

Yeah.

Noble

This is the danger. Atheism is not like that, it cannot be promoted in that way.

Ernest

But why not?

Noble

It just can't.

Ernest

Why not?!

Noble

Oh, for Christ's sake, I am beginning to regret this conversation, Ernest! Would it satisfy you to know that I rather admire your arguments?

Ernest

Thank you, but no, you need to tell me. Why should atheists not spread their truth just as religious people do?

Noble

I needn't tell you anything. It just cannot be that way for athe--

Ernest

Why should there be different rules for atheists? Would you refuse them their *right,* their *freewill,* to spread the truth, for no good reason?!

Noble

Ernest, what is a *right* if it is not man-made or God-given?! What is *good*?!

Ernest

Tell me your reason. Isn't it your job to enlighten?

Noble

Oh heavens, Ernest!

Ernest

Well...

Noble

Okay.
        Wait and I might tell you.

Ernest

Go on.

Noble

Okay. Though, I warn you, my explanation may be a rather lengthy one.

Ernest

That's fine.

Noble

This cannot be told in halves.

Ernest

Tell me. I don't mind.
        I want to hear this. I have nowhere to be.

Noble

And... And I warn you, it may be deeply depressing for you to hear. For atheists, this cannot be unheard.

Ernest

Go *on*, please.

Noble

I will. But first I must make something abundantly clear to you: I am usually quite reluctant to lead atheists to realise the full extent of their truth. You see, it can be rather infectious, Ernest. I've seen it happen before. It can spread like an aggressive tumour and overwhelm a person entirely.

Ernest

Oh, come on.

Noble

No, listen. Nietzsche himself warned against pursuing truths of this kind - as you are. Those that realise the truth rarely emerge from the rabbit hole and those that do, emerge as though it were in reality a badgers den; they return torn and scarred, enfeebled, *different*.

Ernest

Stop dramatizing.

Noble

"There are in fact a hundred good reasons why everyone should keep from it who can" - those were his words. *"For only we, we who keep the mystery, only we shall be unhappy."* This is not dramatizing, Ernest. It is a clear warning.

Ernest

Whatever. Truth is a liberator. It aids the egalitarian fight for universal equality. It fights prejudices and biases and enables technological advancements, and in so doing promotes human welfare. Truth cannot be a bad thing. So, go on and tell me!

Noble

Fine. Since I have warned you and since you still insist on it, I shall tell you. Reluctantly, I might add. Though, I will so only because I fear that the likely alternative is that your belligerence will grow exponentially if I don't. You are in danger of becoming militaristic - if yesterday's events have not proven that already - especially if you believe that you are obliged to share your atheistic truth, Ernest.

Yet, perhaps the only way to defeat your militarism is with Nihilism - which would equate to fighting fire with fire but as you'll soon see there is nothing wrong with that, just as there is nothing strictly *wrong* with anything.

Chapter 2

The Philosophical Atheist

Having now understood Ernest's motives, Noble decides to expose to him the theoretical implications of his manifest militarism, all whilst utilising Ernest's most favoured tools against him - rationality, logic and truth (whatever that is). Noble is firm and tenacious as he begins to reveal the discursive essence of his philosophical character and explains why even the most dogmatic of atheists need God in order to prevent their morals from grievously reducing into moral relativism.

Ernest struggles to penetrate the arguments set before him and, upon realising that Noble too is an atheist, feels betrayed. Despite this, he develops an ever greater need for Noble's approval. With less zeal than before, Ernest continues to make his insistences, now with a glint of rather confused admiration for his counterpart.

Noble

Let's begin then by thinking about the nature of religious conversion. After that we can concern ourselves with atheistic conversion.

Ernest

Fine.

Noble

Okay.

Consider then, for example, when a Christian successfully converts someone. Through converting a person they provide that person with a purpose. That purpose is God or the teachings of God. That purpose provides the person with a degree of meaning - a foundation upon which they can then construct, or indeed modify, their own conception of reality, morality, truth. That purpose, God, becomes a part of their reason to live - that is what I mean by *meaning* - it gives *value,* relevance, to life and the things which inhabit it.

Ernest

Sure.

Noble

Atheistic conversion does not share this characteristic. Especially not for those who are philosophically minded, such as yourself, Ernest.

Ernest

Well, why is that?

Noble

Because the truth is much less desirable than you appear to think. Yet, it is what you are after. So, here we are.

When you convert someone to atheism you don't give them bricks with which to construct their own reality. You are giving them a lethal tool which has the capacity to crush all joy and hope; a tool capable of levelling mountains. Atheism can be utterly disabling, both spiritually and socially and, by extension, culturally.

In theoretical terms, atheism is compatible only with moral anti-realism; and moral anti-realism implies Moral Nihilism. Thus, atheism and Moral Nihilism are, in essence, opposite sides of the same dirty coin. It's just that few atheists ever dare to turn that coin over.

Ernest

Right--

Noble

If atheism were the prince Nihilism would be the pauper.

Ernest

Okay. Slow down. Say that again, but plainly.

Noble

The problem for atheists is that they haven't any moral authority.

Ernest

I've heard this all before but--

Noble

But let me finish.

The problem is not that the atheist cannot *conceive* of right and wrong. I know many atheists, all of them of which are, on balance, equally as honourable as my religious friends. Indeed, they are perfectly capable of conceiving of and following their own moral compasses, be they derived from principles concerning the promotion of happiness or of human dignity, or from virtue. Aristotle, Cicero, Shakespeare, Kant, Mill, Parfit. There are a multitude of the magnificent scholars from antiquity until today from which atheists can develop, derive or intellectualise their own pictures of morality. And non-academic atheists are of course also capable of conceptualising and recognising at the very least rudimentary notions of right and wrong through referring to their conscience. So, there is nothing especially unique about the atheist's ability to conceive of right and wrong.

Ernest

Then what is the issue?

Noble

The issue, Ernest, is that the atheist cannot *justify* her morality.

Ernest

Well, you just said it yourself: they are capable of knowing right from wrong. Why is that not enough?

Noble

Think about it, Ernest. "*God is dead*". That was not a mere seditionary remark; it was not just some paltry provocation. Much more is said than the words. Nietzsche prophesied the inevitable, dire implications of atheism; that if God is not real, then neither is right and wrong; nothing is good or bad. Literally everything, everything becomes meaningless. As I see it, the Earth's death became inevitable the day that God died.

*   *   *

Momentarily Ernest peers around the room. At first he notices an elderly woman wedging her walking stick between the floorboards and the base of the restroom door, holding it open for an obliging youngster. His attention then turns to the bar from which an eclectic cocktail of accents and pretensions are heard well before they are seen: cockiness, cheeriness, merriment, foolishness, propriety, decorum, a flash of banter, wise words, greetings and handshakes at the door. He sees and hears all of this. But he witnesses no piousness, no righteousness, no *religious-ness* - nothing to signify that anyone presently occupying Ye Olde Cheshire Cheese Inn is particularly religious, maybe with the exception of Noble. And yet, everything is in order. Perfect order. A man waits patiently to be served. Giving thanks, a lady places a five-pound note into the tip jar. A waiter sets the tables in the dining area - knives on the right and forks on the left. Everyone appears to be doing everything pretty much just *right*.

Ernest

Sorry, Noble, I'm not really sure I follow you. I mean, I think I do, but this is pretty abstract and unfamiliar territory for me. It seems quite obvious to me that atheists *can* conceive of right and wrong quite easily, as you have just said.

Noble

Yet the truth seeker, the philosophical atheist, who seeks to *justify* her conception of right and wrong will only ever search in vain before collapsing to her knees a failure. Such a justification can never be found, because it doesn't exist. Hence, whatever her moral convictions are, however principled she may be, there is no good *reason* to have them. At a fundamental level, morals are nothing but arbitrary. Atheistic morals that is. Atheistic morals are vacuous - devoid of reason, logically irrational - regardless of their apparent utility. They may appear firm and integral from the outside but in reality they are precarious and weak, much like the subsiding Houses of Parliament.

Yet, your own spiritual position is established more on the idea of scientific truth than it is of religion. Am I not correct?

Ernest

You certainly are.

Noble

A *sound* foundation, yes?

Ernest

I would say so.

Noble

Yes. See, that is your paradox, Ernest. If you insist on the truth - on what you perceive to be *rational* to believe in - then merely conceiving of right and wrong is surely not good enough is it? You, surely, must know *why* right is right and wrong is wrong, no?

Ernest

I suppose.

Noble

You must *know* it?
Correct?

Ernest

Correct.

Noble

So, I should continue?

Ernest

Yeah, go on. I see no harm in it.

Noble

Then I will--

Ernest

If I am so paradoxical, then tell me what 'the truth' of my atheism really is.

Noble

I will. The truth is this: for theists, moral laws are believed to be in some way *out there*, as it were. They are objective, mind-independent, universal truths - meaning that they exist in all possible worlds and are true regardless of how, or if, we perceive them. For theists, moral laws exist because - according to them - they were created by God, the Setter of Standards.

Who sets the standards for an atheist such yourself, Ernest?

Ernest

Mm. I Suppose I do.

Noble

I think not.

Ernest

Well, I think I do.

Noble

Okay. Have I ever informed you of my own faith?

Ernest

No. You're painfully too professional for that.

Noble

It may then surprise you to hear then that I, like you, am an atheist. Who sets the standards for me, Ernest?

Ernest

You are?

Noble

Indeed I am.

Ernest

Then why do you side with Father Chance?

Noble

I do not *side* with anyone. I am merely trying to encourage you to think. For, as you so poignantly put a moment ago, that is my job is it not?

Ernest

Mhm.

Noble

So, who sets the standards for me?

Ernest

Fine. Well, yourself, obviously.

Noble

According to you then, everyone sets their own standards?

Ernest

Yeah.

Noble

And that seems okay to you?

Ernest

I don't see why not.

Noble

I see. Have you never disagreed with someone over a moral issue, Ernest? Have you never debated over corporal punishment, eugenics, euthanasia, abortion, nationalism, slavery, activism?

Ernest

Yeah, of course.

Noble

Do you not see that if it were okay for everyone to set their own moral laws, then moral arguments such as these could never be won or lost?

Ernest

I suppose.

Noble

What is it then that makes, for instance, activism good, or slavery bad? What *is* 'good'?

Ernest

...

Noble

You see, there are no satisfactory answers to these questions. Unless, that is, there exists some kind of Moral Law Creator, a God, a Setter of Standards, to give answers to them; something that can lend reason to, and thus enable us to *rationally* justify, our moral judgements.

Frederick Coplestone won this debate decades ago, some seventy years ago in fact. Frank Turek and Ravi Zacharias to this day are still attempting to elucidate his reasoning, yet few atheists are aware of it, and the fewer that care to listen dare not to acknowledge it. Probably because they are unable to find any suitable counterarguments to it - which is because they don't exist.

Ernest

Well, that seems like a fairly sweeping judgement.

Noble

Does it? Do you believe in morality?

Ernest

Of course.

Noble

You must therefore believe in moral laws?

Ernest

I suppose that follows.

Ernest

Well, then. As a person who believes in moral laws - or moral *truths,* if you will - you must posit a Moral Law Creator, because if there is no such thing as a Moral Law Creator, then there can be no such thing as moral laws.

Anything could qualify as good - even cannibalism or infanticide - if the only authority we can rely on for what good and bad is, for what right and wrong is, is ourselves. --

Ernest

Fine! I don't see why it has to be *God* though.

Noble

Ah! But I'm not arguing in support of God's existence: *God is dead.*

I am simply highlighting that without God there can be no moral laws *per se.* That is, there can be no justification for our morals - no universal moral laws to base our moral judgements and actions on. The atheist who believes in moral laws, contrary to the founding tenets of atheism, is *irrational.* The alternative, if we are indeed in search for and choose to accept the truth, Ernest - as *philosophical* atheists - is that *moral laws simply do not exist.* Otherwise, we, you, atheists, everyone must concede that God is alive and real.

Ernest

Okay, well what about human flourishing? I believe that human flourishing is good in itself. God doesn't need to enter the picture. What about that?

Noble

Aha! Yes. Well. The recent employer of this term appears to me to have injected it with subtleties designed to differentiate it from 'well-being'. However, the subtleties are fruitless; they're redundant when it comes to rebutting your claim. But that's beside the point--

I might add, I know from where you have borrowed this idea: a prominent *militant* atheist nonetheless. And it must be said that his shifty attempt at disguising 'flourishing' as something it isn't failed the very day it was published.--

Ernest

Sam Harris.

Noble

Yes.

Ernest

And I quite like it. It makes complete sense to me.

Noble

Indeed.
Mill claimed that the only thing desirable was happiness.

Ernest

Yes he did.

Noble

This, for Mill, meant that *rightness* amounted in some respect to happiness. He believed happiness to be good in-and-of-itself, and as such doing right equated to promoting happiness as much as possible. No need for God.

Ernest

Well there you have it!

Noble

Ah, but Mill was incorrect. He didn't believe he was incorrect, of course - hubris. However, he was not militaristic like you. He readily admitted that his idea was unprovable. He said it himself that "*no reason can be given for why happiness is desirable except that everyone desires their own happiness*". In short, happiness is good because people desire it.

Ernest

But that doesn't seem at all problematic to me. That seems perfectly reasonable in fact. I said 'flourishing', though. What about that?

Noble

But wait. Who or what decides or determines that something is morally good simply because everyone desires it? *God*?

Ernest

Of course not.
I see.
I think I'm beginning to see your point.

Noble

Good. Whether it's cashed out as happiness or flourishing - or even duty - arguments like this are all flawed.
Interestingly, Kant committed the same crime. He thought, to put it crudely, that since *everyone* values their own rationality, rationality must be intrinsically valuable. So, thinking about it, both Mill and Kant must have believed that morals are mind-dependent - a ridiculously inconsequential notion, if I may say so, for moral laws can't be both universal and mind-dependent. That just doesn't make sense. Otherwise, as you now know, they must have been religious and have grounded their theories in theistic, mind-independent frameworks. They were, or at least Kant was, religious - the verdict is still apparently out on Mill - but they did not ground their moral theories in religion.-- Mind-dependency does nothing to avoid the nihilistic reality.

Ernest

Okay, okay. Slow down. Can't we agree that the promotion of human flourishing is at least a decent concept for an atheist to adopt?

Noble

Perhaps we can. Though, again, let's consider what is meant by *decent*. By 'decent' I presume you mean *valuable*?

Ernest

Well, I didn't choose that word because it has any special meaning. But, now I think about it, I suppose you are right, yes.

Noble

What would you say that you meant by 'decent'?

Ernest

I agree with you: valuable. Intrinsically valuable.

Noble

Ernest, I have just explained that nothing can be intrinsically valuable without there being a God to make it so.

Ernest

No, you highlighted that nothing can be intrinsically *good* without God.

Noble

What is 'goodness' if it is not synonymous with the idea of value? Surely they are one and the same.

Ernest

...

Noble

Let me try to explain in another way.

Chapter 3
Ethical Instrumentalism

Brick by brick Noble continues to dismantle Ernest's intellectual foundations, the fundamental ideas upon which his conceptions of reality and morality rest. By steadily ratcheting the torsion between those ideas and his own, Noble compels Ernest into reluctantly admiring his theses. The Fallacy of Superiority and the theory - or rather the atheological *truth* - of Ethical Instrumentalism are now the subjects of Noble's exposition.

Noble

If we attempt to remove ourselves from our own perspectives and try to look at the world through an objective lens we see that nothing is valuable intrinsically, or mind-independently. Value is merely a relative concept. By this, I mean that nothing is valuable *in-and-of itself*; things are only ever valuable *for-the-sake-of* something else.

Take gold for instance. Gold is not intrinsically valuable. It's only valuable because men decide it is. Without us, gold would probably have no value, meaning that it is not valuable *in-and-of itself*. Because being valuable *in-and-of-itself* would require gold to be valuable in its own right, regardless of how humans qualify it. So, gold is in effect valueless, universally speaking.

Ernest

Yeah, I see what you mean. But gold *is* valuable for monetary purposes.

Noble

Indeed. It's valuable *for* monetary purposes; for economic purposes. Imagine a world uninhabited by humans, devoid of sentient beings, without an economy. In such a world, would gold necessarily have value?

Ernest

I suppose not.

Noble

Good. It certainly would not. Then the essence of intrinsic value is approximately this, Ernest: *something is valuable in-and-of-itself, which is to say 'intrinsically valuable', if and only if it is necessarily valuable in all possible worlds and contexts.* Thus, if you can identify just one possible world, or context, wherein something is not valuable, then that something is not intrinsically valuable. It could still possibly be valuable *for-the-sake-of* something else - which is to say 'instrumentally valuable'. It's just that it isn't valuable *in-and-of-itself*. Gold and money are good examples of this, as we have just agreed. In theological parlance: *for anything to be intrinsically valuable, a deity must exist to judge it so.*

Ernest

A Setter of Standards.

Noble

Yes, there you have it. For anything to be intrinsically valuable, a Setter of Standards must exist to make it so.

Ernest

I had never thought about it like that until now.
I admit, that is an interesting thesis.

Noble

What about diamonds, cars, education, social status, hygiene, health, wealth, ethnicity, sexuality, power, knowledge?

Ernest

What about them?

Noble

Since now you've realised the worthlessness of gold, what do you think of these things - diamonds, social status, wealth, et cetera - all the things on which people tend to mistakenly pride themselves?

Ernest

Well, they are all obviously pointless, if you are right.
I need to think on it.

Noble

Yes you do.
Ask yourself the question: are there any conceivable possible worlds or contexts in which these things are not valuable? If the answer is yes, then they are simply not intrinsically valuable-- I am tempted to say, *according to logic*.

Ernest

Well, diamonds, I suppose the same as all material things, are similar to gold in the respect that they are valuable only because we humans consider them or make them valuable.
And Kant's notion of personhood as being intrinsically valuable is flawed according to your logic, seeing as rationality can't be valuable in a world that has no rational persons inhabiting it. I would guess that for rationality to be intrinsically valuable there must be a rational Eternal Being. But this seems odd. I'm not sure I agree but I see exactly what you mean: it appears that nothing is truly valuable *in-and-of itself*.

Noble

Hence, human flourishing is not 'decent', as you so put it. Because if human flourishing was decent, that would suggest it was valuable, but nothing is truly valuable.

Ernest

Yeah, true. The logic does appear to point in that direction but that doesn't mean that human flourishing isn't better than other notions of good does it?

Noble

Ah, but Ernest, nothing can be *better* per se, can it? If something was better, that is to say intrinsically better than something else, that would be equivalent to saying that it has more intrinsic value, would it not? Yet, nothing has any intrinsic value - if there is no God to give it value - so nothing is truly *better* than anything else.

Things are only better *instrumentally*. By that I mean for-the-sake-of something else.

Ernest

Okay, fine. So, human flourishing is better instrumentally. That sounds just fine to me.

Noble

A car is a car only insofar as it serves the function of being a certain kind of vehicle, correct?

Ernest

Yeah.

Noble

And one car is *better* than another - instrumentally better, that is - because either it serves that function more effectively or because it has an added function or functions. For instance, greater comfort, a stereo, or power steering, and so on?

Ernest

That seems reasonable.

Noble

An elevated social status is better simply because it affords a person more opportunities in life; greater freedoms, if you will?

Ernest

Yeah.

Noble

Rather than, that is - as many people perceive - conferring upon the person some ineffably mysterious token which in some impossibly abstruse way makes the person more valuable in-and-of-themselves?

Ernest

Yeah, I suppose.

Noble

Would you agree that the same is true of wealth and knowledge, perhaps talent too?

Ernest

I would, yeah.

Noble

Then you are beginning to understand.

The problem I fear is that the word 'better' is commonly perceived and utilised to indicate the greater intrinsic value of one thing compared to another. When someone says 'better' that is what is typically meant. Yet, as we have seen - as atheists, without a God, without a Setter of Standards - intrinsic value does not exist. So labelling something as *better* in this way is the same as labelling it as *worse*, for neither terms have any meaning in a godless world.

No car, no house, no lifestyle is any better or worse than another. The rich are no better and no worse than the poor. One person is no better, no worse than any other person. No ethnicity is better or worse than any other; no sexual orientation is better or worse than another. No belief, no *religion*, is better or worse than another. And the same could be said of all things. For, for us atheists, there is no God to settle upon such judgements. This is the Fallacy of Superiority. Things are only better, are only valuable, and are thus only good, bad, right or wrong, *instrumentally*. In reality, there is nothing superior or inferior to anything else.

Ernest

You are right. I understand.

Noble

Therefore, seeing as nothing is intrinsically valuable, or *better*, it follows naturally that nothing is intrinsically *good*. So, now do you see the fruitlessness of human flourishing? Do you see its arbitrariness?

Ernest

I suppose I do, yeah.
    I agree. I think I fully understand you now.

Noble

Good.

Ernest

So, what do you call this thesis of yours?

Noble

Ah! Yes. Well, in honesty it is not strictly *my* thesis. I think Beihl named it, but I'm not sure. It is sometimes referred to as Ethical Instrumentalism.

Ernest

Right.

Noble

Interestingly, it is not really a new theory either. You know, this line of thought has long been ignored by many mainstream contemporary scholars. But if you were to read Arrian's Enchiridion for instance, you would see that Epictetus made an almost identical point nearly two thousand years ago. David Hume alluded to it too.
    And Moore's Naturalistic Fallacy also points to it - he spoke about how judgements concerning intrinsic value cannot be derived from the *"bare facts"* of the world.

Ernest

Interesting.
    It's frustrating that this isn't taught in schools or colleges. Atheists deserve to know the implications of their beliefs.

Noble

Ah, but I couldn't disagree with you more, Ernest.

Ernest

Why's that?

Noble

I only decided to tell you this because I fear that you are becoming militaristic.

Ernest

You did say that you *liked* my argument.

Noble

Yes, in a way I did.

Ernest

Well...

Noble

I don't believe that atheists necessarily deserve to know the implications of their beliefs - the *truth* of them.

Ernest

Yeah, well, why are militant atheists special to you then?

Noble

Ernest, what really is valuable about truth?

Ernest

Like I said before, it helps people, it makes society more equal. For another thing, it leads us to greater technological advancements, it aids progress.

Noble

Oh for heaven's sake! You are really not thinking about this at all are you? Progress to what exactly? What is *progress*? I might agree with you in some respects but I certainly don't *absolutely* agree. The danger for militant atheists, as with all other absolutists, is that they are absolute. Which is to say that they, like you, neglect to caveat their words and thoughts with relative quantifiers, with scepticism - everything is certain for you.

Ernest

But--

Noble

But nothing is certain. As with anything, the instrumental value of truth is only *relative*. That is it's truth is valuable only insofar as it helps people, or makes society more equal. Hence if truth leads to the opposite - to suffering, hatred or inequality or whatever - it's surely not valuable is it? Unless, that is, you would agree that truth is 'valuable' also insofar as it disables people and tears society apart; insofar as it helps society regress?

Ernest

But in what world would that ever be the case?!

Noble

What?! Why, but in this very world!

*　　　*　　　*

Just like an economic bubble on the brink of bursting and inflicting untold collateral suffering, human civilisation has inflated vastly beyond its means and, in the not-too-distant future, is destined to rupture and implode. Anthropogenic human extinction *will* occur, whether as a result of nuclear fallout, a man-made contagion, or - what's most likely - the climate and ecological meltdown. These things have harmed people, are harming people, and will invariably continue to harm people. The victims are many and their numbers increase exponentially by the day. And humanity's capacity to inflict such immense harm upon itself only exists *because* of 'truth'; the kind of truth upon which 'progress' has until now been heedlessly justified - scientific truth.

Noble wants to say all of this and more, but refrains from doing so, instead deciding that a more tactful, less inflationary, more philosophical approach is required if he is to successfully convince Ernest to change his mind.

Noble

I think you're conflating truth with the principles of science, Ernest. *Some* scientific advancements might lead to the things you just mentioned, but *truth*, truth is a very different thing. If truth, like everything else, is merely instrumentally valuable, then you surely understand that there must be some circumstances in which truth is *not* beneficial.

Ernest

Well, yeah, like lying to save someone's life.

Noble

Okay, yes. But I mean *intellectually*. Surely you understand that there must be circumstances when truth is not intellectually beneficial?

Ernest

I guess. Maybe.

Noble

Does that not follow from the logic?

Ernest

Well, maybe.

Chapter 4

The Pernicious Paradox

Noble takes his philosophising to new heights. Now, with greater enthusiasm and a sterner expression, he goes from enthralling Ernest to combating him in an instance of undignified albeit necessitated condescension. In a mission to explain the theories just divulged he goes on to reveal the underside of atheism's 'dirty coin', Moral Nihilism. In doing so, he finds it necessary to explain what he calls the Pernicious Paradox - the struggle which philosophical atheists face upon realising the equal yet irreconcilable realities of Moral Nihilism and Franklism.

In an unlikely twist of character, Ernest is humbled. Cracks appear in his confidence as his passion wanes. Discontented, he cedes the intellectual ground and a new, slightly enfeeble, *different* Ernest begins to emerge.

Noble

You previously accused me of being dramatic. Have you never heard of Nihilism, Ernest?

Ernest

I have.

Noble

Then what does it mean to you?

Ernest

Well, one might refer to a soulless person as a nihilist; someone without morals. Someone who is dispassionate or apathetic.

Noble

Yes, it is true that some people might be described in such a way, but I believe that the employment of the term in that frame is not a fair reflection of Nihilism. Though, I would agree that the word does carry some rather sinister connotations.

Given your depth of understanding in other areas, and your manifest desire to remain rational - whatever that really means - I must admit that this gap in your knowledge surprises me. Nihilism really is the plague of today, yet you clearly know nothing about it.

Ernest

Well, it's never really been a subject of study for me.

Noble

Which I suppose in some ways makes sense. For I am almost certain that if you were properly familiar with Nihilism your tenacity unto now would have waned long ago.

I presume that you have heard of Albert Camus, and Jean-Paul Sartre, Bertrand Russell, or... J.L. Mackie perhaps?

Ernest

Yeah, of course.

Noble

They all attempted to shine a light on Nihilism. Their works are practically ignored in mainstream education. They tend not to be taught until university, at which point their ideas on the subject are rarely given any serious attention.

Ernest

Well, what I can say is that I know that Nietzsche was a nihilist, and Hitler too if I remember rightly. I realise that you respect Nietzsche, and I might not be in a position to fully appreciate why but surely Nihilism's association with Nietzsche and Nazism is enough to put you off a little?

Noble

No, not in the slightest.

Ernest

Okay. Well, I have never been properly introduced to Nihilism and I have never really been inspired to research it myself.

Actually, I have never really thought about it. I suppose I always just assumed that I knew what it was.

Noble

Would you change your mind about it if I told you that Hitler was not actually a nihilist?

Ernest

Maybe. Although I do remember hearing or reading something somewhere that Hitler was heavily influenced by Nietzsche. Isn't that true?

Noble

Perhaps in some ways it is. However, not in the way you might think; not in any meaningful way.

The relationship between Nietzsche and the Nazis is actually a rather interesting one. And contrary to popular belief Nietzsche stood in firm opposition to the Nazis.

Ernest

That doesn't sound right.

Noble

Yet it is true.

Ernest

...

Noble

Perhaps I should tell you first about what Nihilism is before we start wandering down the byways of history.

Earlier you accused me of being dramatic. I'd like to show you why I may have seemed so.

Ernest

Okay, then. We've come this far. Go ahead.

Noble

Nihilism is the product of what we have explored so far: why atheists must accept that moral laws do not exist; that nothing is intrinsically valuable; and that that which is valuable is so only instrumentally, and that this is called *Ethical Instrumentalism*.

Nihilism is not an ideology; it has no axioms, tenets or principles. It is merely what the philosophical atheist observes, whether or not she sees it; it is, in essence, simply the atheological reality. Hence Nazism cannot be based upon it. Do you understand?

Ernest

Yeah, I understand that Nazism cannot be based upon something that is not an ideology, but I don't understand how Nihilism isn't an ideology. Actually, even if it isn't an ideology, it could still have greatly influenced or inspired the Nazi ideology, right?

Noble

Yes. Very true, Ernest. Very true. Yet it is not and it did not.

Let me tell you about the seriousness of what we have spoken about so far. The Russian writer and philosopher Fyodor Dostoevsky - who you may or may not have heard of but whose novels have been the subject of high academic study for almost a century now. Dostoevsky was bemused with how an atheist could know that God does not exist and yet not commit suicide. He really could not understand it. I, however, am almost sure that many people *have* committed suicide because of Nihilism. It's not that they reflect upon it in their journals or mention it in their suicide notes, nor that they divulge it to their GPs or psychiatrists. Perhaps they never really see it, or perhaps they do but can't quite put their finger on it, can't quite rationalise it. All the same, they are possessed by it. It does that, you see. It has a medusan effect; upon seeing it you become forever stuck. This is the seriousness of Nihilism. It has killed and it continues to kill. It has many unsuspecting victims. It inspires people to commit suicide and others to murder. I would argue that it's what corrupted the USSR's attempt at communism. It is the consequence of a godless world; a world without morals, value and meaning.

Ernest

A world without *meaning*?

Noble

Yes, indeed.

Ernest

I don't understand.

Noble

Think about it. If nothing is valuable in any relevant sense - if nothing is *intrinsically* valuable - then what is the point of, for example, pursuing a career, or sponsoring a charity, marrying a partner, receiving an education? What is the purpose, the meaning?-- Why bother?

Ernest

Well, all of them have a purpose.

Noble

Do they?

Ernest

Obviously the purpose of a career is to help us live well, build capital, gain status. And the purpose of giving to charity is to do good, or make someone's life better. The purpose of marriage, romantically anyway, is to make a public declaration of your bond. And the purpose of an educati--

Noble

Yet, none of that really makes any sense if nothing is valuable does it?

Ernest

I'm not sure I agree with that.

Noble

What is the purpose of status - be it social, financial or professional - if no one's status is truly *superior* to anyone else's? What is the purpose of earning more than one's competitor, more than a merely humble living, if the goods one resultantly purchases are themselves devoid of any intrinsic value and excess capital is equally intrinsically worthless? What is the point of 'doing good' by giving to charity if 'goodness' is just an illusion? What is the point of sport, of power, of happiness, of *life*, if nothing is meaningful in any relevant sense? For that is the logical implication of a moral-less, valueless world, is it not, Ernest?-- That everything is meaningless and nothing is meaningful?

We spoke a moment ago about the Fallacy of Superiority and the material things that people identify by - class, ethnicity, wealth, et cetera. You realised that no class, no ethnicity, nothing, nothing is superior to anything. Well the same holds true for the abstract. Happiness is no better than depression, consciousness no better than automation, virtue no better than vice, goodness no better than depravity, life no better than death.

Ernest

...

Noble

In order to obtain any semblance of contentedness our unconscious requires that the objects and events which inhabit our lives, as well as the actions we take, are meaningful; we require them to be relevant. Once we realise that nothing is intrinsically valuable that relevance disappears; there is no purpose, no meaning to anything.

It does however follow that certain things, modest lifestyles for instance, free from any significant financial woes, are *instrumentally* better for those fortunate enough to have them. Yet, beyond the instrumental benefits of wealth there is clearly no intrinsic value to it. Nor, for that matter, is there any in success, charity, romantic exclusivity. Alas, there is not even any value in a PhD...

Ernest

Fine.

Can you repeat what you said a moment ago, though, about meaning.

Noble

If you need to hear it again... of course.

Every pursuit we ever make, in its own way, must be considered meaningful, even if only subconsciously, for us to retain any passion for it. Yet, once an atheist realises the truth of their reality, that is once they realise *Nihilism* - that nothing is intrinsically valuable, that nothing is valuable in any psychologically relevant sense - then all passion is lost. For they realise that nothing in their lives is meaningful. Depression and psychosis, perhaps even psychopathy, infect the individual and, through them, begin to invade society. In the words of Russell, *"the cosmos is alien and inhuman and the values we cherish have no realisation in it."*

Ernest

Okay...

Noble

Perhaps I am muddying the water a little. Let me attempt to make things clearer. I, erm...

I firmly believe that Viktor Frankl spoke the truth when he said *"man's search for meaning is the primary motivation in life."* His idea was strongly inspired by Nietzsche's - that someone can bear almost any amount of suffering if they have a sufficient reason to live. At the very least a person needs to have a *will to meaning*, a desire to find meaning. Without either meaning or the will to meaning, they are bound to suffer an existential crisis, depression, and their overall well-being will rapidly diminish. Hence, the foundational requirement for well-being is *meaning*. Call this thesis Franklism.

If you're ever tempted to read Frankl's work you'll realise that it has convincing empirical foundations. Which are vividly described, I might add. Indeed some of it is truly difficult to read. You see, Frankl survived the holocaust. He lived, or rather subsisted, in Auschwitz ,and wrote his theory subsequent to both witnessing and personally experiencing some of the most extreme and industrial forms of persecution and suffering. He retells multiple examples of how prisoners who somehow found meaning amidst that hell on Earth were able to outlive those who had lost it. All he and his fellow inmates possessed, he said, was their *literal naked existence*. However, the very few that survived the holocaust did so through somehow finding the remnants of something absolutely vital to human existence, something alien to most of their comrades that died. That something was *meaning*. By inconspicuously taking up roles, as rabbis, doctors, teachers, or by holding on tight to the hope that God might one day reward them for keeping faith, few succeeded in evading death. Those that lost meaning suffered a *"kind of emotional death"* from which the will to live rarely ever returned. And this was almost inevitable since apathy was the only method of self-defence available to them in their moments of absolute vulnerability. Frankl noted how some prisoners lost their fear of the gas chambers, because being gassed to death spared them the act of having to commit suicide.

Ernest

Wow.

Noble

He was undeniably a most incredible man. The strength, the courage, he must have had in order to reflect upon and then to study those experiences was surely enormous. The whole thing is almost unfathomable.

Ernest

Yeah.

Noble

Now, we philosophical atheists face a problem, don't we? The problem we face is marrying two incompatible truths. The first truth is that, as we have just seen, humans fundamentally require meaning in order to live. The second is Nihilism; that the universe is in reality entirely valueless, and therefore devoid of meaning - which, admittedly, is absolutely terrifying.

But, in short, to fully exist the philosophical atheist requires something that does not exist. In other words, Franklism is not consistent with Nihilism, and this is the paradox the philosophical atheist is destined to realise and bound to suffer from, Ernest: an existential *Pernicious Paradox* if you will. That is what I've taken to call it anyway.

Ernest

Erm... Well, I really don't mean to reject Frankl's observations, but if you would qualify me as a 'philosophical atheist' then I am proof against your paradox because I am certainly *not* suffering from it. Maybe the pursuit of reason and scientific truth gives me meaning!

*　　　*　　　*

Taking a sip from his beer Noble begins to look a little uncomfortable but ploughs on, vigilant to any creeping reappearance of Ernest's characteristic pugnacity. Almost instantaneously he weighs the pros against the cons of pushing Ernest to fully realise the moral implications of his atheism, judging that Ernest's absolutism, his militarism, his *bigotry*, ought to be quelled at all costs, for the sake of anyone who might otherwise fall victim to it such as those at the bible study group the evening before.

Noble

Perhaps! Yet rationality is not as valuable as you think, Ernest. You are lying to yourself if you believe that truth should always be sought after. It doesn't deserve to be put on a pedestal and worshiped as an ideal. Indeed, surely you can see now that lies, or at least misunderstandings, are absolutely necessary for the atheist to experience a meaningful and peaceful existence.

Ernest

No. Sorry, what? You're saying that irrationality is *beneficial*?

Noble

Yes! That is what I'm saying. To be a contented atheist you cannot believe in the truth absolutely, but must sometimes believe in lies. For the philosophical atheist to find any semblance of meaning in their nihilistic world they have to be, to some extent, irrational. Do you not see? You criticize theists for being irrational - which they may indeed be. But irrationality is just as much a necessity for atheists. You have already agreed, we have nothing upon which to justify our values and judgements. Yet we hold on to them nonetheless. Why? Because our irrationality is what makes us human. Irrationality is instrumentally valuable for us, Ernest. Otherwise, we philosophical atheists truly are *"condemned to be free"*, condemned to suffer the Pernicious Paradox. Or, perhaps, that is what you are avoiding, Ernest, if you do not agree with me.

Ernest

I am avoiding nothing. You said that you were trying to make me think and that is what I am trying to do. You also said that you'd tell me the truth and I have stayed to listen, only because I believe in the importance of rationality. So, I can't accept that irrationality is a good thing, regardless of what you say.

Noble

I'm not claiming that irrationality is valuable *in-and-of-itself*. I'm claiming that sometimes, just *sometimes* - so that atheists can believe in morality for instance - sometimes irrationality is instrumentally valuable. I can try to explain again, one last time, if I really must?

Ernest

...

Noble

Sartre once said that religion takes people's freedom away from them for their own sakes: "*a religious person is conscious of being free to sin, but is not free to decide what sin actually is*." Similarly, Dostoevsky stated that religion, for that very reason, bestows upon its followers "*blessings of happiness*". For orthodox Christians the divine command is absolute; unquestionable. They needn't worry themselves with the project of testing it. That's none of their business. For them, ignorance really is bliss.

Yet, with respect, Ernest, atheists such as yourself, who remain attached to *truth,* are forgetting that you are not, like those Christians, shackled by religious absolutism anymore. That *blessing* does not apply to you. No, atheists are free to dare, to intellectually explore the reality of morality themselves. Moreover, they are free to question the very existence of morality altogether!

Ernest

But--

Noble

Either that or atheists are so immensely fearful of what with their newly discovered freedom they might find that they abstain from their freedom to think, which, ironically, is not very rational now is it Ernest?

Ernest

Ye--

Noble

I appreciate how frightening it must be for atheists. It frightens me too. Atheists easily become lost; at odds with themselves; petrified even. Especially once they realise that they no longer have the warrant nor the psychological ability to perform that blissful Kierkegaardian 'leap of faith'. For 'faith' carries no meaning for them! To what would they leap?! They long for the ability to leap to the other side, but they no longer stand at the precipice peering across the void to a brighter, more blissful world. No. They live in the void.

    You must realise this, Ernest. You have no warrant to have faith in rationality, or truth. For *the truth* is that truth is not always a beneficial thing to possess.

    I fear I am getting carried away with myself. I apologise but I can't say it any clearer. Nothing - not even truth - is intrinsically nor absolutely valuable, nor good. Things, all things, are only relatively valuable; valuable instrumentally. The universe is essentially meaningless, Ernest.

Ernest

Fine...

Noble

I am sorry. This is as plainly as I can put it.

Ernest

Yes, and I have heard you now, loud and clear.

Noble

And now you can see why it's dangerous to be militaristic, to try to convert people to atheism? This is what I meant when I said that I believe militant atheism is immoral. As an instrument it can be completely disabling.

Ernest

Yes, I realise now.

Noble

You did insist on the truth.

Ernest

I did.

*   *   *

Noble presently realises he has committed the very crime he warned Ernest against doing, of ignobly imposing the reality of atheism upon others. Guilt throbs within veins as he seeks to reconcile with what he has done before solemnly leaving Ye Olde Cheshire Cheese Inn for a cigarette. Ernest waits, sitting on the cusp of apathy's event horizon, peering down into the deep, dark den of nihilistic introspection but is brought back to reality upon Noble's return.

Noble

I apologise for my bullheadedness.

Ernest

No need. I now properly understand.

Noble

> I know, but I am sorry. I shouldn't have...
> > I am sorry.

Ernest

> It doesn't matter. You succeeded in your mission to help me understand. I was looking at truth abstractly, as an objective. I realise now that you have given me *the truth* and, admittedly, I can see myself soon wishing that I hadn't heard it.

Noble

> Yes, but I went too far--

Ernest

> No, I suppose you are correct, Noble.
> > I will have to think all of this through, thoroughly.

Noble

> Yes.

Ernest

> You have opened my eyes. So, I guess... I guess I should apologise to you.

Chapter 5

The Importance of Meaning

Having conceded a lot of ground already, Ernest finds it difficult to accept Noble's claims regarding Franklism. Nevertheless, Noble persists in his endeavour, and after making several attempts to expose to Ernest the damaging consequences of militantism, Noble unwittingly makes a personal admission of his own apathy. Explosive and rather undignified, Noble outbursts with his agony, unveiling an element of his personality which Ernest had only received fleeting glimpses of before.

Until that very moment, and contrary to his typical character, Ernest appears borderline indifferent, seemingly unwilling to argue much longer as he mulls on the implications of the Pernicious Paradox.

Ernest

Noble.

Noble

Yes?

Ernest

Erm... I think I'm beginning to see... that there aren't any mind-independent moral laws to base my convictions on anymore. Maybe I don't hold those convictions anymore. I don't know, I'm not sure.

But, about Franklism. I was thinking. Maybe happiness is more important, like instrumentally, than meaning when it comes to human well-being. What do you think? It's just that, maybe, meaning might lead to happiness and that's why it is important to have it. Would you agree?

Noble

I believe that without meaning no one can attain true and
lasting happiness. And that is assuming we know what we
mean by 'happiness'.

Ernest

Right, okay. Well, yeah. Pretend we know what we mean by it.
In which case wouldn't you say that happiness is of more
importance to well-being?

Noble

No, I don't think I agree. Do you believe that there is a difference
between happiness and well-being?

Ernest

Not really. I think that happiness pretty much just is well-being.

Noble

So for you a person's well-being amounts to their level of
happiness?

Ernest

Yeah

Noble

In which case then I disagree.

Ernest

Why?

Noble

Well-being and happiness are very separate things. More
importantly, I believe that meaning is of fundamental
importance to human well-being.

Ernest

More important than happiness?

Noble

Yes. Certainly.

Ernest

Fine. Well, I'm not reluctant to admit defeat, but I really think that you have this one wrong.

Noble

That's fine.

For me, human well-being and happiness are clearly distinct ideas. A person's level of well-being is determined by their physical and mental health. Happiness, among many other things, can promote a person's well-being, and can thus be seen as contingently beneficial, but our well-being does not necessarily require happiness. However, human well-being necessarily requires meaning.

Ernest

Sure, but in what way?

Noble

Ah, indeed. Good question: *in what way?*

Derek Parfit explored what a 'life worth living' might amount to. In all honesty I can barely remember properly what he wrote but the notion is crucial here: 'what makes a life worth living?' is a central question in understanding well-being. The answer according to Franklism is *meaning,* and I believe this to be the correct answer. Actually, I have mulled over this for quite some time and would make a distinction between a *life worth living* and a *good life.*

Ernest

Right. Interesting.

Noble

A *life worth living* is the very minimum we require in order to be willing to live, whereas a *good life* is what we can aspire to only if we have a life worth living. So, one can have a life worth living regardless of whether their life is good but they cannot have a good life, or in other terms *live well,* without their life being worth living. Does that make sense?

Ernest

Yeah.

Noble

Great. So, I would define a *life worth living* as a life with, at the very least, meaning. *Living well* is defined as having both meaning and a suitable level of welfare. This is what it means to be *contented*: to have meaning and a suitable level of welfare. Hence, it follows that for life - and for human well-being - meaning is more important than happiness.

Can you see how happiness and well-being are distinct in this picture?

Ernest

Yeah, I think so. In your paradigm human well-being consists, at first principle, in what is essential for human life.

Noble

Indeed. Whereas in your paradigm human well-being consists in happiness.

Ernest

That's right.

Noble

So, the way I see it, you have approached things backwards. You started your reasoning from the top - from what makes people flourish; from what makes people *live well* - and then you worked your way down. When what you should have done was work from the bottom, from what is *essential* to life, from what makes a life worth living, and then work your way up to what makes us live well.

Ernest

I see. Yeah, maybe you're right.

Noble

I have an example which I think you might find more convincing.

Ernest

Go on then.

Noble

Consider a man who is in the hospital dying from an incurable terminal illness. He is in excruciating pain. The pain is so pervasive, so severe, that no amount of medicinal pain-relief is able to considerably reduce his suffering. He is, by definition, the opposite of happy; his level of well-being is *almost*, though not completely, unendurable. For, he is experiencing the greatest amount of physical suffering a human can reasonably endure, and suffering is the converse of happiness - correct?

Ernest

Yeah, agreed.

Noble

Yet, this man is deeply in love. Let's say he is in love with his children and with his wife. And he loves the world for having enabled him to find love and be loved. Love gives him meaning, purpose; it makes his life worth living. That is what meaning is, remember. Meaning makes a life worth living.

So, when the doctor consults the man about whether he'd like for his life to be prematurely euthanized, to put him out of his suffering, the man cries *'no! I have everything still to live for!'* because his reason to live remains stronger than his reason to die.

Ernest

Okay.

Noble

Now, imagine another man. A truly flourishing man. He is perfectly healthy, without any ailments whatsoever, fit even, and handsome. He has everything he could ever wish for in life. All the material possessions anyone might desire. He travels frequently, he is social, practical and creative and has status and power, both financially and professionally. Yet, in spite of everything, *meaning* evades him - perhaps, like us, he is a philosophical atheist. Devoid of meaning and incapable of finding any purpose to his life, he begins to believe that his life is not worth living. And as Frankl said, *once lost, the will to live seldom ever returns.* Eventually, he loses even the will to *find* meaning, gives up and commits suicide. Why?

Ernest

Because he was depressed.

Noble

Yes. He is entirely unhappy, but only precisely because he could not find meaning in his life, despite all of his riches. Do you see, Ernest, that the first man was suffering but wanted to live, and the second was suffering but wanted to die?

Ernest

Yeah.

Noble

Does this seem like a realistic example?

Ernest

It's definitely conceivable that both cases could be true, yeah.

Noble

Good. So, meaning makes all the difference. If you take away a man's meaning, you take away his will to live; you risk making his life not worth living.

This is why I told you about Nihilism. Militant atheists fail to see that for some people their faith, their religion, is ultimately what gives them their identity; it is what gives them meaning. For some people it is the *only* thing that gives them meaning. But that meaning is inherently valuable in making their lives worth living. So, if that meaning is taken away - if they are berated into abstaining their faith - then their spirits are effectively murdered, Ernest. Trust me, I know this to be all too true.

Ernest

Okay.

What do you mean?

Noble

I have thought this scenario through many times before and I often feared myself to be that second man.

Ernest

But what are you saying?

Noble

...

Ernest

What do you mean?

Noble

Oh, no. No, sorry. I don't know why I said that.

Ernest

Seriously? What do you mean?

Noble

No, really, we needn't talk about it-- But if Viktor Frankl's case isn't relatable enough for you, take it from my example, meaning really is the bedrock of well-being.

Ernest

Yeah but Noble, you can't just say something like that and expect me not to be concerned or ask questions.

Noble

No, Ernest. Please. Thank you for your concern but really there is no need--

Ernest

I mean, you can talk--

Noble

No, no. There's no need.

Ernest

You shouldn't act so professional all the time. A problem shared is--

Noble

Is a problem doubled.

Ernest

Is a problem halved...

Noble

Ernest, please. I've revealed enough of the truth to you. I needn't also unveil the existential repercussions of knowing it. Given your character you'll undoubtedly realise them yourself, and I really do not intend on leading you there. So, please, let's move on.

Ernest

Yeah, but surely you're intelligent enough to understand that suppression is not healthy--

Noble

Please Ernest--

Ernest

Yeah but you--

Noble

No---

Ernest

You *must* talk to someone--

Noble

I know very well, Ernest!-- I know very well! But the truth of Nihilism is that unless one suppresses it or has a religious epiphany it is *incurable*!

Ernest

Er--

Noble

However, I am not suppressing it-- I am very aware of it!-- It eats at me like a plague-- I see Nihilism *every day*: in the naive smiles and fragile ambitions of my undergraduates, in the perfectly ironed shirts of the City's service professionals; I see it at the cinema, on the sports fields, in the lecture theatres, at the bloody matinee! It's fucking everywhere, Ernest!

Ernest

I--

Noble

But the good news, Ernest-- the good news is that I *see* it. I should be thankful for that-- Those of us that experience and are concerned by the Paradox are those that remain human - it means we still possess a conscience. So I am relieved to suffer! It's those that see it who don't suffer that go on to do barbaric things.-- I am still human and as long as I remain human I will refuse to infect anybody else with the truth, not even a fucking psychiatrist!

Ernest

But--

Noble

Like I said, it is medusan. You *do* know who Medusa is?!

Ernest

I--

Noble

I think I need another drink. Would you like a drink?-- I'm getting a drink.

Ernest

I, I'm sorry.

Chapter 6

Nietzsche, Nihilism and the Nazis

Noble leaves for the bar, giving Ernest relief and time to ponder on the implications of their conversation once more. With his thoughts bouncing from topic to topic - Atheism to Instrumentalism, Nihilism to Franklism - Ernest is incapable of suppressing his hectic mind.

How did he fail to sense Noble's fragile condition? Throughout their entire conversation he had been completely transfixed by his own perspective and the challenges raised against it. So much so that he'd neglected to consider the roots of Noble's ideas; neglected to realise that Noble himself is a victim of the paradox that he'd warned against - the *Pernicious Paradox*. Some way, somehow, Ernest is convinced that amidst everything he might find a way to bring Noble peace, if only he can find the right logic, a convenient argument, a new way of thinking. Sitting, deliberating, having now capitulated to Noble's philosophy, he rocks back and forth on the rear legs of his chair, waiting out this second interval in their doomful discussion, procrastinating, reluctant to accept his own perniciously paradoxical fate, searching for a philosophical remedy to Noble's psychological ailments.

With both now experiencing forms of nihilistic turmoil, Ernest and Noble scale down the gravity of their discussion, shifting away from the ostensibly pernicious and abstract subject of meta-ethics and towards the comparatively concrete subject of history; or, to be specific, the history of Nietzsche and the Nazis.

Ernest

Cheers.

Noble

Let's move on. God forbid we should speak about something a little more cheery.

Ernest

Okay, sure.

Really, though. I am sorry.

Noble

No, no. Let's move on.

Ernest

Fine.

Tell me about Nietzsche.

Noble

Ha! Joyous!

Yes. Okay. I can't deny that that is at least a *little* lighter a subject, and I did want to show you that my appreciation for Nietzsche does not make me a Nazi-sympathiser.

Ernest

Yeah, well I never assumed that, but I guess with what you've told me so far this evening that other people might.

Noble

Yes, regretfully some people do.

But I have to admit, I am not at all an authority on Nietzsche. Like most people, my limited knowledge concerning him and his ideas relies heavily on the works of Walter Kaufmann. Though, I do believe his works are credible.

Ernest

Okay.

Noble

I said earlier this evening that the supposed association between Nietzsche and Nazism was false.

Ernest

You did.

Noble

Okay. Erm, I presume you'll not be leaving any time soon?

Ernest

Well, the drink you just bought me suggests I'm staying at least a little longer. Thanks, by the way.

Noble

Right, Yes. You're welcome.

Okay. Nietzsche and the Nazis then...

According to Kaufmann - and I believe Hollingdale mentioned this also - the false association between Nietzsche and the Nazis constitutes a part of a legend; a seemingly everlasting legend, the *legend of Nietzsche*. This legend is so prevalent, and his style of writing so uniquely labyrinthine, that discovering Nietzsche's thought is seldom a leisurely pursuit. But *studying* it reveals a thinker entirely detached from, albeit related to the legend.

Ernest

Mm.

Noble

From what I have read, Nietzsche's legend is generally considered a work of fiction.

Ernest

Interesting. But if this legend you speak about isn't true then why is it still going?

Noble

That is a good question, Ernest. Some years ago Stephen Hicks wrote a documentary about Nietzsche and the Nazis which I think answers that question rather well. In his documentary he made a fairly simple yet quite accurate assessment of western society's broadly held associations between historically significant political revolutions and the prominent thinkers of their times. For example, Hicks suggested that we make an association between the Communist Revolution and Karl Marx; he said that when we think about the French Revolution we consider Rousseau; and that when we think about the American Revolution we consider John Locke. It's difficult to gauge whether this is entirely true - I am certainly no anthropologist or historian - but it is definitely a credible idea. With that said, what Hicks was trying to highlight in this thesis was that none of these thinkers had any direct involvement in their associated revolutions and that often their ideas were hijacked and indeed completely corrupted by people who sought to use them to intellectually justify their own political ends.

Perhaps because of certain things to do with his legend, the thinker nowadays most commonly associated with and cited in relation to the German National Socialism revolution is Friedrich Nietzsche.

Ernest

I can believe that. That definitely sounds like a credible theory.

Noble

Also, legends have a tendency, don't they – through the creation of stereotypes, euphemisms, hyperbole, not to mention the quite human inclination to embrace and embellish legends and subconsciously will them into reality – they have a tendency to be self-perpetuating.

Ernest

Yeah.

Noble

So, yes, the legend persists still today but it only really exists in fictional literature, in films; or perhaps in unread, idiomatic conversations. The academic consensus on this is quite clear: the Nazis were wrong and/or ignorant in their appropriation of Nietzsche.

Ernest

Right. But the Nazis *were* inspired by him?

Noble

Yes, they were but, as I said before, not in the way you might think.

Okay, so here is an example of how Nietzsche's name tends to precede him. As you are probably aware, it is generally believed that in his younger years Nietzsche was rather unsanitary. He was by all accounts a recluse, but regularly dabbled in narcotics and frequented brothels to which his contraction of syphilis is attributed. And, be it that this predated the advent of antibiotics, towards the end of his life he supposedly became insane as a result of and eventually died from the disease. His legend is notorious in this regard. I'm sure you know this much at least?

Ernest

Yeah, I've heard something along those lines before. Didn't his insanity influence his writing style?

Noble

Perhaps. Perhaps his ailments, or his drinking habits, affected the way he wrote. In reality, however, other things caused him to go mad. He didn't actually have syphilis. He had cancer. However, these spurious anecdotes about syphilis and his unconventional writing style fit very well with his legend don't they? So well in fact that they appear to have stuck to it.

Ernest

Well. Yeah. Interesting...

Noble

Kaufmann made this observation in the 1950s. Yet, here we are some seventy years on still talking about Nietzsche's syphilitic madness. Humans really do love a legend, a story, a stereotype. We cannot help it.

Ernest

I know near on nothing about Nietzsche, but the one thing I thought I knew was that syphilis caused him to go mad.

Noble

Indeed. You are our proof of his legend then.

Ernest

Mm.

Noble

There's more. During his later years, his sister, Elisabeth Förseter-Nietzsche, pursuing her own ends, began to shape the social and political perception of Nietzsche. She was extremely wealthy, involved in statecraft and politics. She effectively curated the Nietzsche legend. And her legendising of him was ramped up after Nietzsche's eventual death.

Because of his background and notoriety, the Nazi Party quickly followed suit and - as he was no longer alive to state otherwise - they eulogised Nietzsche as their ideological saint, espousing a false version of his supposed 'philosophy' in a PR stunt designed to intellectually legitimize their political ideals and their eventual genocidal actions.

As the figure most responsible for the creation of the Nietzsche-Nazi association, Elisabeth Förseter-Nietzsche is said to have repeatedly invited Hitler to visit Nietzsche's archive. It is also said that Hitler proudly used Nietzsche's walking stick whilst exploring Elisabeth Förseter-Nietzsche's newly inherited estate.

So, I suppose in some respects the Nazis appropriated Nietzsche.
They certainly utilised some of Nietzsche's written aphorisms, but these were far removed from their original contexts and thus falsely represented. Indeed - I vividly remember reading this - in one Nazi publication Nietzsche is quoted as saying that *"the stock-exchange Jew is the most revolting invention of mankind."*

Ernest

Oh god.

Noble

Indeed. This deplorable anti-Semitic phrase was used as intellectual propaganda, favouring the eugenical extirpation of the Jews.

Ernest

Ah, wel--

Noble

But. But they left out what immediately follows in Nietzsche's original text; that being Nietzsche's suggestion that in very many other respects *humanity* is *deeply "indebted to the Jewish people"*. Perhaps Nietzsche left his writing open to misappropriation. Perhaps it is bound to happen when someone of such a reputation writes in such an aphorismic way. Furthermore, perhaps we could condemn Nietzsche for being so inflammatory; we may even conclude that he is personally to some extent blameworthy for the misappropriation of his writings. After all, even if his intentions weren't anti-Semitic, his words were and he lived in an extremely febrile political era, much like our own, and he knew that. Yet, despite all of this, importantly, this should not detract from the fact that Nietzsche clearly did not condone Nazism and neither did he condone all the revolting things that went with it.

The Nazis wrote books - *books,* plural - containing Nietzsche's Nazi teachings, by cherry-picking aphorisms and phrases or by changing his words and taking them out of context. They were all lies. Just like his sister, they counterfeited Nietzsche for their own ulterior motives. Yet, unfortunately maybe, their missions were successful weren't they? For the legend of Nietzsche lives on, as you yourself can attest.

Ernest

Yeah.

Absolute power corrupts absolutely.

Noble

Yes! Indeed it does.

Interestingly, It doesn't take all that much to realise that in reality Nietzsche would have been opposed to the ideologies created under his name. Indeed, he openly and unequivocally denounced Aryanism *and* Anti-Semitism. Furthermore, he branded nationalism and race hatred as - quote-unquote - *"a scabies of the heart"*.

Ernest

Wow.

Noble

Yes. Well, his style of writing was undeniably extreme but he was far from the extremist his legend implies he was.

Ernest

But, maybe, Nietzsche's Nihilism – the meaninglessness and valuelessness and such - maybe that in some way influenced the creation of the Nazi ideology? That could be possible.

Noble

I can see why someone might think that. But I do not think so.

Nihilism was never Nietzsche's theory *per se*. Rather, his writing on it was an empirical description of the world he witnessed. It was a description of what a darwinised, increasingly scientific world was likely to realise; he spoke about 'the elephant in the room'. Indeed, it arguably remains the elephant in the room today. Like I said, few atheists dare to turn over that coin. Whether or not Nietzsche's decision to *reveal* what he witnessed was wise or responsible is a separate issue - and an issue I am currently at odds with personally. However, one might believe that he had good enough intentions and wrote about Nihilism to warn humanity about what he predicted would inevitably take place in a godless world.

That the Nazis then commandeered this message and used it as a call to arms is unquestionably one of the most fraudulent and reprehensible political manipulations in modern history. Indeed, no one with even a vague understanding of Nietzsche's work and the philosophy of Nihilism could judge that the Nazis went to war, or that they institutionalised genocide, on the *basis* of Nihilism. Wars cannot be justified on the basis of Nihilism. I'm not entirely sure that Nietzsche realised it, but nothing can be justified on the basis of Nihilism, as you now know. For the nihilistic void provides nothing on which to base anything - everything simply falls into the void, nothing stands, nothing gets nurtured, nothing grows.

Ideologies such as Nazism, by definition, require a degree of moral absolutism in order to exist. But Nihilism - as we have seen - plainly highlights, or rather recognises, that nothing is morally absolute. Moreover, it tells us that moral truths simply do not exist.

Ernest

However, whilst ideologies, war and genocide can't be validly based on Nihilism, they can result *from* it can't they? They can result from those in power being possessed by it?

Noble

I don't think so.

Ernest

Really? Why?

Noble

Look, I'm not entirely sure on this Ernest, but assuming Hitler was a nihilist, given that he couldn't have thus had any absolute moral convictions, his ideology would have merely been a front – a way for him to covertly enact his nihilistic psychopathy. On the other hand, I would think that the academic consensus on this is that Hitler *did* possess absolute moral convictions. Indeed, I would not be afraid to propose that he had some of the most fervent moral convictions imaginable. The consensus is that Hitler was probably a depraved psychopath, but he evidently wasn't a *nihilistic* psychopath.

Ernest

Mm. Right, okay. That kind of makes sense I suppose.
As much as I think I'm beginning to appreciate your logic and everything you've said, there is one thing I am finding it difficult to reconcile.

Noble

What is that?

Ernest

Well, if according to Nihilism nothing is strictly morally wrong, or *bad*--

Noble

According to *atheism* nothing is strictly wrong or bad, Ernest. Remember atheism and Nihilism are effectively the same thing.

Ernest

Fine. Sure. Well, if you believe in Nihilism and if nothing is strictly morally wrong according to Nihilism, then for you and Nietzsche the holocaust wasn't a bad thing. But obviously you don't think that do you? Of course the holocaust was bad, right? The holocaust was probably the most depraved event in human history--

Noble

I completely agree. The holocaust was a dark and wretched abomination.

Ernest

So you can see the contradiction between that and what you have been saying?

Noble

Absolutely. I acknowledge the contradiction. And I am yet to find a suitable answer to it, other than perhaps that my inability to believe in moral truths together with my apparently 'moral' convictions might simply be an expression of my own Pernicious Paradox.

I definitely see good and bad in the world, Ernest, but, as I have already shown you, when I follow the logic, none of it is recognisable as 'moral' per se. I don't deny my contradiction, though. And, believe me, it frequently and deeply troubles me that I've not been able to find a solution.

Ernest

Yeah, it really is a problem. Surely morality exists, even if only ethereally.

Noble

It certainly *feels* that way, but the logic tells us otherwise. Has what I've said so far this evening not been convincing? Have I not been logical?

Ernest

It seems that you have.

Noble

I think so. Rest assured, however, there is no need to assume that being a nihilist necessarily leads one to becoming nasty and brutish any more than anyone else is bound to become nasty and brutish. The nihilist certainly doesn't by necessity condone the holocaust. True, for the nihilist the holocaust was not a morally bad event. However, it also follows that for the nihilist the holocaust was not a morally good event either. And this isn't a case of fence sitting. Morality just doesn't exist according to the nihilist, so neither does good or bad. Hence, neither I nor Nietzsche thinks the holocaust was *morally* bad. But, fundamentally, we passionately believe - or at least I know that *I* passionately believe - that the holocaust *was* bad, tremendously bad. Indeed, it was positively disgusting, just, not in a moral sense.

As yet I am unable to discern the sense in which it was bad. Though I am certain that it wasn't morally bad. For I am an atheist, like you, Ernest. And that makes us amoralists: for us morality does not exist. Yet, I would reiterate that this doesn't make us any less compassionate, loyal, loving, duty-bound or conscientious, does it? It doesn't make us any less human.

Ernest

Right.

Noble

So, now you can see that being an admirer of Nietzsche need not imply that I am a heretical Nazi-sympathiser?

Ernest

Yes. Well, you're not a Nazi-sympathiser at least.

Noble

Haha! Yes.

Ernest

I doubt our conversation could be called anything but heretical.

Noble

I doubt it could be.

Ernest

Noble...

Noble

Yes?

Ernest

Nietzsche was a quite unfortunate man really, wasn't he?

Noble

That he was...

I have long believed that he must have suffered immensely upon realising Nihilism. To teach it, to write about it, is to suffer it.

Ernest

Maybe he experienced his own Pernicious Paradox.

Noble

That is just it. Maybe he did. I expect so.

Ernest

If what you say is correct, then towards the end of his life...

Noble

Indeed. And considering he had cancer too, he must have had a deeply depressing existence, especially towards the end.

*　　　*　　　*

As the pair finish their drinks and ready themselves to leave, Ernest has one final remark to make, one last question in need of an answer. He has an inkling of some other significant atheological truth, of what is to follow, but is unable to trap and interrogate the thought before it escapes him.

Ernest

It's quite obvious to me that you still think and speak in moral terms, Noble.

Noble

Yes?

Ernest

Well, even if you are unable to express the sense in which you understand 'good' and 'bad'. Surely, what you see as good or bad is by-and-large what I see as good and bad.

Noble

Are you sure?

Ernest

What I mean is, it seems that whilst you deny the existence of morality, you still think and speak morally. So, even though you say it doesn't exist, even if the logic of atheism points in that direction, morality still seems to exist for you.

Noble

I see what you mean. You are saying that amoralists are effectively moralists in denial, aren't you?

Ernest

Yeah. I suppose, in a convoluted sort of way, that is what I'm saying.

Noble

We've covered a lot of ground so I can understand why the distinction mightn't be that apparent to you. It is clear though, Ernest. Amorality is distinct from morality because it does not possess the feature of being an instantiation of some special property that is either supplied by the universe or by God. Remember, we have no *reason*, no *basis* upon which to justify our notions of morality. Remember?

Ernest

Ah, yeah, okay. Sure. I see that.

But, I don't know. There is still something. There is something about suffering from the Pernicious Paradox. I can't put my finger on it. If you weren't moral, you wouldn't suffer from it. You wouldn't class the holocaust as bad. Or maybe you would. No. I don't know.

Look... sorry for earlier.

Noble

I should apologise too. I lost myself, more than once.

Ernest

Don't worry.

I should probably get going.

Noble

Yes, well I shall be leaving shortly also.

I truly am sorry, Ernest.

Ernest

Erm. Fancy another tomorrow? Same time?

Noble

Yes, strangely I do. Same time, same booth?-- if it's free.

Ernest

Sure.

Noble

It is conveniently secluded in here. Fairly suitable for conversations concerning religious sedition.

Ernest

Ideal for heretical conversations too.

Noble

Indeed. Stay away from the chapel now.

Ernest

Don't worry. I'll leave Father Chance alone this evening.

Noble

I expect he's still recovering from your last meeting.

Ernest

I expect so.

Part Two
Searching for Salvation

Through discourse and discourse alone, can a person derive a way out of a philosophical conundrum such as Nihilism. And rarely does a philosophical conundrum not translate into a real life problem. In this case, liberation was sought after and (perhaps) discovered in a familiar but now damp, leathered hollow, next to a smouldering, ashy fireplace in the bustling basement of Ye Olde Cheshire Cheese Inn. A place where until now doomful debates have been fought and mostly lost, even by those who've won, and especially by any atheists who've paid close enough attention. So, if you have come this far, do not let up. In the words of the late Jibreel, as he spoke to Muhammad in the great cave of Hijra, *"Read!"* For, only by reading might anyone happen upon any semblance of a resolution to their inner turmoil; a calming of their cerebral tumult; a release from that decadent internal abyss. And, perhaps a semblance is just about all anyone really needs.

Here, at the beginning of the end, as the world approaches its final conclusion, as the final chapters are observed, words are exchanged that should have been exchanged long-ago between richer, more influential atheists. The question is: can the "*plague of today*" be reduced to a mere cold; to something from which humanity can recover; to more virtuous and less absolute realities; where nobleness and earnestness balance closer to equilibrium; where spiritual opulence succeeds in counterbalancing needless truths?

Before considering whether Earnest and Noble have it in them to answer such a question, it would be wise to revise what has hitherto been revealed about atheism's reality. So, here are the headline features to date: **Ethical Instrumentalism** is the thesis that nothing is intrinsically good; nothing is good in-and-of-itself; x is good only for-the-sake-of y. **The Fallacy of Superiority** is the false proposition or belief that some things are more or less intrinsically valuable than other things; all things are in reality intrinsically valueless; all things are (vacuously) intrinsically equal in value. **Moral Nihilism** is (arguably) a necessary implication of atheism; the belief that morality does not exist; the contention that our ideas of morality do not reflect the amoral reality of the universe. **Franklism** is the thesis that human well-being fundamentally necessitates meaning. And **The Pernicious Paradox** is the logical contradiction between Moral Nihilism and Franklism; an expression of the cognitive dissonance resulting from consciously discovering that the universe is inherently meaningless, whilst knowing at the same time that any *life worth living* fundamentally requires meaning; in other words, a recondite condition experienced by some very unfortunate erudite atheists - *philosophical* atheists.

Chapter 7
Prudentialism

Woeful and bedraggled, tentatively shaking the rainwater from his saturated cotton blazer, Noble attempts to warm himself by the fire after stoking it with his boot in a miniature rage. As he settles into the same entombed cubicle from where his and Ernest's doomful discussions took place the evening before, he peers around the Inn to begrudgingly witness some of its drier patrons smirking at the watery trails leading the way to his leaking presence.

Quite the opposite in both his appearance and demeanour, and darning an impressively sleek and efficient hooded-raincoat ubiquitously sprinkled with rapidly evaporating beads of dew, Ernest soon follows, setting two pints of ale upon the uneven, and now rain-sprinkled table. Still concerned with how he might enable Noble to find a similitude of happiness, Ernest decides to get straight to it.

Ernest

Oh good, it's free.

Noble

Bloody climate change. If I knew we were going to get winter in summ--

Ernest

By the way, I saw Father Chance again this morning.

Noble

Excuse me?

Ernest

I decided I wanted to speak with Father Chance again.

Noble

What?! Are you honestly telling me that after everything we spoke about yesterday, after your prejudicial tirade about the narcissistic nature of God, you went back to that chapel?--

Ernest

Yeah, but--

Noble

Did I not advise you to leave that poor man alo--

Ernest

Yeah, but calm down, you don't understand.

Noble

I think I do.

Ernest

No, no. You don't! I went back to apologise!

Noble

You... You did?

Ernest

Yes! I went to apologise.

Noble

Oh.

Ernest

On my journey home yesterday I, I felt... well, regretful is the word. Honestly, I saw the remorse in your face, after you told me about the nihilistic implications of atheism. You made me realise why it's important not to be militant and, well, I just felt like I had to find Father Chance to apologise. So I did. He was incredibly gracious.

Noble

Ah. Well. In that case, I apologise. Very well done.
Perhaps you'll find salvation yet. Cheers.

Ernest

Ha! Yeah, cheers.

Noble

The Father is a pious man.
    So, what did you say to him?

Ernest

Well, I told him that I was lost, but that now I am found.

Noble

Oh, Ernest!

Ernest

What? I did! I said that I had spoken to a friend about my
actions and that he'd guided me to a higher truth, and that I
was sorry. He wasn't very pleased to see me at first, but
appeared to understand the metaphor once I got to explaining.

Noble

Of course he understood the metaphor, you fool. It's from the
Gospel of Luke!

Ernest

Oh. Right. Yeah, I did actually know that. How embarrassing.
    Well, maybe he could tell that I was being sincere or
something. He was very amicable.

Noble

Or maybe he thought that you'd had some sort of spiritual
epiphany. He probably thought he'd witnessed a miracle - a
militant atheist turned evangelist overnight!

Ernest

Well, funny you should say that. After everything we spoke
about yesterday, I felt as though I did have a revelation. Sort of.

Noble

You did?

Ernest

Yeah. The fact that he was so amicable made me feel even more guilty you see, and I couldn't help but feel bad about pressuring you last night too and, well, that got me thinking. Yesterday you mentioned the conscience.

Noble

Er... I did? I can't remember.

Ernest

Yeah. You said that you are relieved to suffer as a result of the Pernicious Paradox because it proves to you that you're human.

Noble

Ah. Okay...

Ernest

I realised that the conscience is vital in all of this. It's because of our consciences that we nihilists suffer--

Noble

Oh, *we* nihilists suffer, do we?

Ernest

Yes, *we* nihilists.

Noble

Right. Very good. Just checking. Go on then, tell me more about your revelation.

Ernest

Mm. Fine.

It's because of our consciences that we suffer and feel guilty about doing wrong, even though we realise that wrongness doesn't really exist in reality. I realised that the Pernicious Paradox is just another expression of the perennial battle between human reason and emotion. Maybe, in a sense, for those who experience it, it's an overwhelmingly crippling paradox. But in another sense, it's just another part of our nature - our human nature.

Noble

Okay.

Ernest

Have you heard of Prudentialism?

Noble

Er, yes. I believe that I have. I think that I read an article or two
about it once upon a time. Why do you ask?

Ernest

Okay, so I read up on Nihilism last night. Come to mention it, I
barely slept, so apologies if I don't get my words across very
well. But I researched what some people have done to try to fix
Nihilism and I think that Prudentialism could be your answer.

Noble

You do?

Ernest

Yeah.

*   *   *

Noble is relieved not to see Ernest bogged-down by his self-acclaimed
revelation, and proud to discover that he apologised to Father Chance
following yesterday evening's discussions. He'd felt guilty for forcing
Ernest to realise the moral implications of his then staunchly rationalistic
atheism, and became deeply concerned that he'd effectively murdered
his spirit. Yet, here he is - the same diligent and enthusiastic Ernest. Well,
not entirely the same Ernest. By his very nature, he still exudes a vague
yet shameless foolhardiness. But he's less obstinate now, not as steadfast
as before, and apparently vacant of bigotry - for the most part anyway.

Despite this, Noble recognises the symptoms of someone who's
delved into an intellectual rabbit hole and worries about the state Ernest
will be in when, or if, he finally emerges. Because of this, he decides to
investigate the musings of his student, to gauge his status on the

existentialist spectrum, to ensure that Ernest hasn't been entrapped by Nihilism's snare. For, Noble thinks Prudentialism could be a dark and narrow tunnel to venture down.

Noble

Tell me, in what way? I'm sorry to say this but I'm not sure that it is the answer, Ernest. But... but I could be wrong.

Ernest

Well, from what I gather Prudentialism effectively allows us to continue being moral, but in a nonmoral way.

Noble

I see.

Ernest

It's action-guiding too. Since we can make sense of actions harming or benefiting us, we can make sense of *ought*-claims; claims that tell us that we *ought* to do this, or we *ought* to not do that. They aren't strictly *moral* ought-claims, but they are ought-claims all the same.

Noble

Prudential-oughts, rather than moral-oughts.

Ernest

Yeah.

Noble

That is a nice and logical distinction. Though, I think what you mean to say is that Prudentialism provides an ethics.

Ernest

Yeah that's what I mean.

Noble

Which is not to say that it necessarily provides us with any guidance on morality, Ernest.

Ernest

Really? Well, what's the difference?

Noble

Ethics and morality are quite distinct.

Ernest

Right.

Noble

Morality purports to inform on goodness and badness. Whilst an ethics is more like a prescribed code of conduct; it defines the appropriate ways by which we can determine our actions.

Ernest

Right.

Noble

To put it briefly, ethics is generally action-guiding, whilst a morality without an ethics attached to it isn't.
Morals might tell us what is *right*, but they don't necessarily tell us that we *ought to do* what is right. Although, one might argue that that is implied. Anyway--

Ernest

Okay--

Noble

Unfortunately, I don't think Prudentialism allows us to continue acting morally.

Ernest

Yeah, okay.
Well, I don't think that's necessarily an insurmountable problem, especially if Prudentialism implies that we ought to act as though morality is real. Which is how I understood it.

Noble

Ah. Interesting.

Can we pick that idea apart a little bit?-- Because at the moment it's not entirely clear to me what you mean, though it certainly does sound interesting.

Ernest

Yeah, sure.

Noble

Okay. I have a question, then. Why is it bad to be 'bad' according to Prudentialism?

Ernest

Err, I don't understand. What do you mean?

Noble

I mean, why is it prudentially bad to be or do what you would traditionally consider to be morally bad?

Ernest

Erm.

Noble

Don't worry-- Let's clarify, though: what is 'bad' or 'good' according to Prudentialism, as you understand it? What is 'prudent'?

Ernest

Right. Well, I suppose prudence is acting in whatever way advances a person's interests. For example, being polite, or according with the law, or, as I just mentioned, acting in a way that most people would consider *right*.

We are benefited by doing these things. Which means that it is in our interests to do them - it's *prudent* to do them - because if we get along with people, it makes our lives easier.

Noble

Okay, I see. However, it'd be rather narcissistic for us to premise our ethics on the basis of what advances only our individual interests, wouldn't it, Ernest?

Ernest

   ...

Noble

Yesterday you were concerned when you discovered that I don't consider the holocaust to be an immoral event, weren't you?

Ernest

Yeah. But you *do* see it as wrong, just in a nonmoral sense.

Noble

Yes, you are right. I do see it as wrong.

However, all things considered, I think it would be fair to judge that my life hasn't, in any relevant sense, been affected by the holocaust. For I'm not of Jewish heritage and, from what I understand, no one of my family or friends were impacted by the holocaust either. So, how am I supposed to judge the holocaust, Ernest, according to Prudentialism, given than it neither benefitted nor harmed my interests?

Ernest

Erm. Well, I'm not sure.

Noble

Neither am I, which I think is problematic.

But look, the question I'm considering is this: does what is *prudentially bad* always match up with what we might traditionally consider to be *morally bad*? And, I don't think it does. Which is important, because you said that Prudentialism advises us to act as though morality is real.

Ernest

   ...

Noble

Prudentialism is acting in whatever way advances one's own interests, correct? Or, conversely, acting in a way so as to avoid harming one's interests?

Ernest

Yeah.

Noble

And you said that it is prudent to act morally. That is, for the sake of my interests, I should act according to morality, correct ?

Ernest

Yeah.

Noble

According to *what* morality, Ernest?

Ernest

I'm not sure I follow.

Noble

There are many different moralities.

Ernest

Well I suppose according to the most popular morality, the one that most people would consider to be right.

Noble

Ah! Consider the holocaust again, then. If the Nazi guards at Auschwitz, for example, murdered thousands of people in cold blood but had managed somehow to avoid self-harm - if Germany had won the war, for instance - then *for them* there would have been nothing *prudentially* wrong with their actions, according to your definition of Prudentialism. After all, they adopted the prevailing moral ideology of their culture at the time.

Ernest

...

Noble

There's a problem there, isn't there? Because your own notions of morality, prior to discovering Nihilism, judge their actions to be wrong regardless of any additional facts - regardless of whether Germany lost or won the war - correct?

Ernest

Er, yeah.

Noble

So, do you still want to say that it is prudent to act in a way that most people would consider right, even if their conception of rightness is overtly morally wrong according to your own conscience?

Ernest

No. Of course not. Fine, it's prudent to act in a way that most people would consider right, provided it doesn't contradict with one's conscience. Is that better?

Noble

No, not at all. Many of the Nazis wanted the Jews dead! Many nationalists genuinely felt that their complete eradication was the only suitable answer to the 'Jewish question'. Their actions conformed with what their consciences told them was right.

Ernest

Okay, okay! Let me simplify Prudentialism then. Erm...
          Prudentialism is simply acting in a way so as to promote one's interests. That might mean that sometimes it is prudent to act in a way that most people would consider morally right.

Noble

I'm not sure that works either, Ernest.

Ernest

Well, why not?

Noble

What about, say, rapists and murderers? What if a rapist or psychopathic murderer managed to live unsuspected by society? Provided they don't stir suspicion and don't get caught, it seems as though their depraved actions advance their interests. Is it therefore *prudent* for them to rape and murder?

Ernest

Well obviously not.

But maybe then Prudentialism isn't about immediately and wistfully advancing one's interests. It could also be about risk avoidance. I mean, it's highly likely that a serial rapist or psychopathic murderer would eventually get caught.

Noble

So, it's bad to rape and murder, according to you, simply because there is a risk of getting caught; because there is a *risk* of one's interests being harmed?!

Ernest

Erm. No.

Noble

What if the chances of getting caught are slim? Do you know how many rape cases result without charges in this country? I read about this in the Times a few months.

Ernest

...

Noble

It's about ninety per cent. Ninety per cent of all reported rapes go uncharged. Does that make it prudent to rape, should one so desire it?

Ernest

No! Of course not.

Noble

Have we not fumbled our way back to something analogous to moral relativism here, Ernest?

Ernest

Mm--

Noble

Except, in this instance, we could refer to it as 'non-moral' relativism, given that it is based in the understanding that morality doesn't really exist.

Ernest

Er--

Noble

You see. Prudentialism appears to condone morally-undesirable acts - acts that the *consciences* of most stable-minded, upright people would find entirely deplorable.

There is also the very grave possibility that Prudentialism might discourage people to challenge - or, conversely, it could encourage people to buy into - uncivilised and regressive ideals and cultures, because it states that people ought to avoid harming their own interests, and rarely is it in anyone's interest to be a victim of discrimination, to be outcasted, or ridiculed.

Ernest

What do you mean?

Noble

What I mean is... What I mean is, for example, if Prudentialism was prevalent in the nineteenth and twentieth centuries, the progress western society then made in terms of prejudice and discrimination arguably might never have happened. Women, foreigners, homosexuals, people with disabilities, would all still broadly be considered as less deserving and less valuable people, and treated as such.

In uncivilised cultures, where individuals are denigrated, assaulted or, worse, murdered, for speaking out, for whistleblowing, or overstepping an invisible social line, for activism or martyrdom, or for identifying as something unpopular - the ethics of Prudentialism, as you have explained it, would suggest that those victims were blameworthy for what happened to them, and that the culprits had only done what should have been expected. What a horrible world it would be if *victims* of discrimination were condemned and the culprits condoned!

It's the kind of ethics that exacerbates social divisions, and, well, this is just speculation, but I wouldn't be surprised if it has implicitly existed in various quarters of society as an unspoken rule for a very long time already.

So, those who've had the courage to disobey it ought to be praised. In tackling prejudices and society's ill, those brave activists - the suffragettes of the past and the climate activists of today - all acted against their own interests. They put themselves in the line of fire, to help promote a world where everyone, despite their differences, can find meaning and peace.

Ernest

Mm, yea--

Noble

What would happen to democracy, if Prudentialism was prevalent? It seems to me that Prudentialism is the sort of ethics that the far-right, that extremists of all colours rather, would like society to adopt; and the sort of ethics that encouraged German citizens to become so complicit with Nazism. It's the sort of ethics employed in a state of nature, when life is *'nasty, brutish and short'*. The sort of ethics that *civil* society should by definition reject wholesale.

Ernest

Yeah, I see what you mean.

Noble

Good.

It is true that I suffer the Pernicious Paradox, in part because of my conscience - you are correct about that: I cannot reconcile my feelings about right and wrong with the reality that I have discovered, which tells me that right and wrong do not exist. Regretfully for me, you witnessed that yesterday. But I don't think Prudentialism does anything to fix that, Ernest.

Ernest

Yeah.

Annoyingly, again, I think I agree with you. It's too individualistic. Prudentialism probably isn't the answer then.

Noble

Indeed.

Ernest

But...

Well, there's definitely one thing. It's definitely prudent for peop--

Noble

Definitely?

Ernest

Well, yeah, you said it yourself.

Noble

You're veering on appearing absolutist again, Ernest. Be careful.

Ernest

You said it yourself!

Noble

What did I say?

Ernest

You said yesterday that irrationality is inherently valuable for human well-being. You said that it's prudent for an atheist to be to some extent irrational, in order for them to avoid the Pernicious Paradox; in order for them to hold moral convictions; in order for them to continue believing that there is value and meaning in the world; so that they can believe that their life is worth living. You said that.

Noble

Yes. That is true, I did say that. And it is as true for ordinary people as it is for ordinary atheists. But how does that help *us,*

Ernest? We aren't ordinary atheists; we are *philosophical* atheists. We've already discovered the Pernicious Paradox.

Ernest

But Noble, if you're possessed by the Paradox then I think that shows that you're just as obsessed with the truth as I was! Why else would the Paradox bother you so much? You obviously think that the truth of Nihilism is of paramount importance.

You berated me for being obsessed with the truth, but you are obsessed with it too!

Noble

...

Ernest

Ha! See! You told me not to put truth upon a pedestal, but that is exactly what you are doing. You pretend like you aren't, but you are. You can't help but stare into Nihilism's void because you have an intellectual spotlight shining down into it all the time; you can't prevent yourself from staring at it.

Noble

Now you're being ridiculous, Ernest.--

Ernest

Let yourself forget about it once and awhile!

Noble

Oh, come on--

Ernest

No. I'm not telling you to pretend that it isn't real. I'm just saying that you don't have to focus on it all of the time.

Look, if the Paradox is toxic, which it *clearly is*, if it is the *"plague of today"*, then surely it's *prudent* to believe in things which contradict it, even if those things are works of fiction, and even if one has already discovered the truth of morality and value - or the untruth of it, the reality of Nihilism - as you and I have. It's obviously *prudent* for nihilists to believe in fiction too.

You taught me that. I learned that from *you*! But you don't seem to really believe it.

Chapter 8

Giving Credence to the Conscience

Still steeped with youthful diligence and ambition, as yet unshackled by the existential chains and bolts of Nihilism, Ernest attempts to bullishly empower and relieve Noble of his personal Pernicious Paradox. In response, and borderline-awestruck by his student's fresh philosophical vision, Noble swiftly realises that he must abdicate authority over the issue and, rather than tutor Ernest, he must assist Ernest in articulating his thoughts, to usher him and help avert him from falling prey to the Paradox too.

Noble

You're really proposing that I need to forget about Nihilism?

Ernest

Yes! Well, not entirely. But from time to time, yes. If this Pernicious Paradox you speak of results from the equal but irreconcilable facts of Moral Nihilism and Franklism, then I don't think you really have a choice. When, as you said, Nihilism kills, and if meaning is the fountain of human life, then your only option is to do away with Nihilism isn't it?!

Noble

But I can hardly just forget about it, Ernest. Yet...

Yet, perhaps you are right. Perhaps I have unwittingly given precedence to the truth of Nihilism. But I am an academic - or at least I am trying to be. Academia is my chosen path - it's what gives *me* meaning - and it is premised upon me attempting to shine a light on truth. *We* are philosophical atheists, Ernest.

Ernest

Yeah. Well, I'm sorry but I reject the claim that academia is currently providing you with any sufficient degree of meaning - that really is a tenuous remark.

Noble

...

Ernest

I'm sorry. But, couldn't you just allow yourself to forget about Nihilism once in a while? Just momentarily?

Noble

No, I'm not sure that I can.

Ernest

But it's crucial. Isn't it clear that it's absolutely *prudent* that you try, for the sake of your sanity?

Noble

...

Ernest

Well, isn't it?

Noble

Perhaps, it is.

Oh, Ernest. We really have travelled some distance since our conversations yesterday. Yesterday I wouldn't have ever conceived that you'd be telling me to be *illogical*; to throw my rationality to the wind!

Ernest

But I'm telling you to *be* rational. If overcoming the Paradox is about self-preservation, and the only way to overcome it is to omit Nihilism from the picture, then you *must* omit Nihilism from the picture. That's rational.

Noble

> Perhaps it is. Yet, like I said, I am an academic. I cannot just mystically omit Nihilism from my mind.

*   *   *

Noble presently realises that Ernest - now frequently yawning and red in the eyes - seems to have discovered something quite profound in his fatigued state, which from his blinkered perspective, from within the darkness of the void, Noble was unable to see. Hence, partly as a gesture of admiration, and partly in an attempt to reconcile the potential harm he exposed his compatriot to yesterday, he decides to subtly guide Ernest, to give his ambitious ideas direction and set them on a trajectory far away from nihilism's gaping oesophageal vacuum.

Noble

> However.

Ernest

> Yeah?

Noble

> I'm willing to concede the possibility that you might be right.

Ernest

> Really?

Noble

> Yes.

Ernest

> Oh, wow. Okay.

Noble

> On the assumption that you are right, it *might* be prudent to qualify Moral Nihilism as a secondary principle; i.e., a second-

order principle.

Ernest

Okay. Well, what do you mean?

Noble

As you suggested a moment ago, out of the two principles which culminate in the Pernicious Paradox - i.e., Franklism and Moral Nihilism - Franklism is more important to being human, because it tells us that having meaning is inherently valuable to obtaining a life worth living, and the very least anyone needs in life, after their *bare existence*, is to believe that they have a life worth living. Since Nihilism negates Franklism, it may indeed be prudent to give it precedence over Nihilism in our philosophy.

Ernest

Yeah, great. Agreed--

Noble

In this sense, Franklism is a first-order principle and Nihilism is second-order.

Ernest

Right, okay. That makes sense.

Noble

So, to clarify: roughly speaking, ordering the principles in this way is justified on the basis that it is prudent to believe in morality before anything else; it is important to believe in it more than in the value of truth, or the pursuit thereof.

Ernest

Yeah. Agreed. That's what I was trying to say. Truth, like everything - as you said yesterday - is only valuable for-the-sake-of something else. And in this instance, believing in morality, regardless of whether it is true or not, is valuable for-the-sake-of finding a life worth living--

Noble

But we needn't believe in any specific morality. Nor, as we have seen, should we necessarily believe in any popular morality. We simply need to believe in the existence of morality; of our *own* morality. We need to have *faith* in our conscience; to believe that it *can* successfully track rightness and goodness. For, only by doing this might the philosophical atheist, the *nihilist,* find any semblance of meaning.

Ernest

Yes!

*   *   *

At this very moment, in a dazed attempt to sit up and grasp for his pint, Ernest jolts the table with his knee. Noble's drink swiftly burps a volcanic bubble of froth into the air and slides several inches across the water-licked table before its base is intercepted by a sticky knot in the wood, stopping it dead. Almost instantaneously, the top of the glass continues with velocity on a downward curved trajectory, splashing Noble in the face and drenching his already rain-wet shirt in tepid Indian pale ale before then rolling and tumbling onto his lap.

As he waits still drying by the fire, having done all things possible to mitigate his soggy, hoppy circumstances, with the dried and damp parts of his attire blotched like the fur of an old and greying Dalmatian, and with a sodden pile of napkins at his side, Ernest considers how his own conception of the world has recently manifested. He discovers that maybe, perhaps rather absurdly, he has found meaning in the meaningless of the universe. For, the universe's meaninglessness has assured him that all the prejudices in the world, the cultures and the arbitrary traditions, conforming to ancient conservative ideas concerning the intrinsic value of things, are all ill-informed; for there is no intrinsic value to anything. And he realises that he could have thus ignored these prejudices, cultures and traditions, in the knowledge that, morally speaking, they are neither right nor wrong; for neither rightness or wrongness, nor goodness or badness, truly exist. But he didn't ignore them. He couldn't ignore them, because his conscience wouldn't allow it. And that is precisely why he has suffered from the Pernicious Paradox.

Thanks to Ernest, he now sees that what makes him human is that he possesses a conscience, and that *that* conscience tells him - and has always told him - that he ought to try to do right by people. In spite of the fact that 'rightness', when scrutinised, appears to be a philosophically fragile, if not an entirely vacuous, concept. And, on the assumption that most people have a conscience (otherwise, the world would surely be overrun with psychopaths), it follows that philosophical atheists would benefit from assimilating a fictionalist morality; if only so that they can confidently and contentedly react to what their consciences see, even if their minds are blind to see it. The conscience appears to necessitate morality, regardless of whether that morality truly reflects any universal moral laws of nature. And this ought to be respected, if the philosophical atheist is ever to find meaning in life.

As he approaches the bar to purchase Noble a replacement pint, Ernest recalls something that Noble mentioned a moment ago, something important but which his tired mind neglected to cogitate until now, or possibly which his embarrassing fumble distracted him from acknowledging: 'It's important to have *faith* in our conscience; to believe that it *can* successfully track rightness and goodness'. Almost miraculously everything begins to fall into place. The conscience is psychological, he realises. It's a feeling, a personal sentiment of rightness, goodness, wrongness and badness. And that sentiment is felt regardless of one's intellectual convictions. The conscience *forces* us to discriminate between right and wrong, whilst the Paradox counteractively tells us it's illogical to make such discriminations. But you cannot override the conscience, because as soon as a nihilist overrides the conscience they become unhealthy and indiscriminate; or worse, unhuman, anti-human even, maybe even psychopathic. For being fully human requires that we possess, listen to and are *guided by* the conscience. *Yes*! We require that we are guided by the conscience. So, the conscience isn't always guided by our morals and our ethics. Sometimes the conscience drives them!

Ernest

I cannot believe I just did that.

Noble

Ernest, I'm not going to say that I enjoy having beer thrown over me but, seriously, did you not see me before? I was already soaked to the bone.

Ernest

Well--

Noble

Don't worry--

Ernest

I'm never like that.

Noble

It's because you haven't slept. You really should try to get a decent night's sleep, Ernest. Stop concerning yourself with philosophy and let your mind properly rest.

Ernest

You're right. I might have to call it a night after this one.

Noble

I think that'd be wise.
          But let's see how we do. I was just starting to think that we were getting somewhere.

Ernest

Yeah. Me too.

Noble

In fact, I was just about to say that I think you might be right.

Ernest

Yeah?

Noble

Perhaps it *is* prudent to believe in morality, in order to attain any semblance of a life worth living; to prevent us from being permanently tainted by the dissonance that accompanies the Pernicious Paradox.

Ernest

Yes. That's what I was thinking. The Pernicious Paradox isn't as pernicious if Franklism is given favour.

Noble

Indeed.

Ernest

Mhm.

Noble

Having said that...

Ernest

What?

Noble

There is still one thing.

Ernest

And that is?

Noble

I'm still struggling a little to believe that this is practicable, Ernest. I struggle to believe that I am able to entertain fiction - i.e., believe in morality as though it's real. Surely one cannot both *believe* in morality whilst simultaneously *knowing* that it isn't real; that it doesn't in reality track any universal moral law of nature.

Ernest

Well, of course you can! In fact, we all do it to some extent. Any student of ethics can tell you that if they were to rationalise and investigate their own moral convictions, then they would definitely find flaws and inconsistencies within them. Nevertheless, they usually remain moralists don't they?

Noble

I suppose.

Ernest

Of course they do. Actually, most of the philosophy undergrads I know are probably also the most morally aware people that I know. They don't just discard their morals when they discover a problem with them. They might modify them slightly but on the whole they retain them and they continue to act upon on them, because acting morally rarely requires us to be one-hundred-percent cognisant of all the implications of our moral convictions. In most instances where we make moral decisions we aren't at the height of our consciousness. So, in most moral contexts those students believe in their moral convictions, but in more critical contexts - when they are scrutinising their morals in their seminars, for example - only in those contexts might they disbelieve in them.

Noble

I see. So, you're suggesting that I can be a nihilist in moments of elevated criticality?

Ernest

Yeah. Well, no. You can be a nihilist all the time. Only, you needn't think like a nihilist all the time.

Noble

Okay...

Ernest

Listen. You can know morality to be fictional and still make moral claims, and still *think* morally. It's just that you'd withhold doxastic assent from those claims and thoughts; i.e., in moments of elevated criticality - as you put it - you wouldn't believe in them.

In the non-academic areas of your life you can allow yourself to believe in and rely upon the morals that your conscience tells you exist; you can rely upon what your conscience tells you is right and wrong.

Noble

Okay.

Ernest

I'm sure you're able to read fictional novels without accepting them as true, right? But you *entertain* the stories entailed within them anyway?

Noble

Yes.

Ernest

An--

Noble

I see what you are saying. You are suggesting that there is a distinction between belief and acceptance.

Ernest

Erm... Yeah, I suppose I am--

Noble

One can believe something in a non-academic sense without necessarily accepting it as true in an academic sense.

Ernest

Yeah, that's right. We are humans, not robots - we are more nuanced than that.

Look, just as in order to live we tend to deny the reality of our impending and inevitable death, in order to live *well* we have to deny the meaninglessness of the universe. In order to have a life worth living we need to deny the meaninglessness of life.

Noble

That does make sense.

Ernest

Of course it does. It follows from everything you've told me since we began talking about all of this yesterday.

Noble

Yes. I see now.

Yet, I just thought of one more issue that I think it is worth mentioning.

Ernest

Fine. What's that then?

Noble

I'm not entirely certain that it applies. But this idea that we are supposed to give credence to the conscience, as it were - this idea appears to encourage compartmentalisation, which is typically considered to be psychologically inexpedient.

Ernest

And what's that?

Noble

It's a concept in psychology that I came across some time ago. It's used to describe a subconscious defence mechanism which is triggered when someone tries to prevent two contradictory aspects of their life from meeting one another, to avoid having to modify or discard either of them; to prevent the consciousness from being harmed.

Ernest

To prevent cognitive dissonance?

Noble

Yes, indeed.

Ernest

Erm. Well, could you give an example?

Noble

Yes, I think so. Let me think. Er...

Okay. Consider a manipulative but incredibly successful City salesman. The sort of salesman that cheats and cons, who is ruthlessly pragmatic and doesn't much care about the consequences of his work, provided he receives a bulky commission.

Ernest

Okay.

Noble

In this context he doesn't deserve to be characterised as a kind, compassionate or giving man does he? He's neither an honourable or respectable man.

Ernest

Agreed.

Noble

Yet, when he goes home in the evenings after work, he's very different. He is the father and husband to a family that loves him very much, who are immensely grateful for the security, the food and shelter, and all the added luxuries his earnings allow them to indulge in. So, in this context he is an honourable and respectable man; a kind, compassionate and giving man.

Ernest

Right.

Noble

The question the psychologist might ask is: in what light does this man see himself? And that's when compartmentalisation becomes clear to see. For, despite his depraved activities at work, he sees himself in a good light; his self-image is based solely upon the man that he is when he is at home. He compartmentalises - separating, in his mind, his work-life from the rest of his life, so as to prevent himself from having to reconcile with the fact that he may not be as honourable and respectable as he had hoped he was; that he may not really deserve the admiration and appreciation he receives from his family.

Ernest

Right. Okay. That's pretty clear, and I get why compartmentalisation might be considered undesirable in those circumstances - it enables him to go on doing abhorrent and immoral things at work. I suppose a similar example could be drawn about someone who loves their spouse but cheats on them, or someone who donates money to Trees for Life but eats loads of beef.

Noble

Er. Yes. Yes, I suppose so.

Ernest

But our circumstances are unique. If *you* compartmentalised your belief in Nihilism it would help you to resume being moral. By definition, that would surely be a good thing. It wouldn't be inexpedient at all. It's not as though it would lead you down a dark and depraved path. Nor would it cause you to suffer - that you are already doing on your own.

Noble

Yes, okay.

Ernest

Then again, I don't think what we have said necessarily equates to or even encourages compartmentalisation. You *can* believe in morality without accepting it and, at times, accept Nihilism without believing it, as I have already exampled. That doesn't equate to psychological repression or hypocrisy. It just all depends upon your present level of criticality.

Noble

I understand. And I think I agree with you.

I still think that for people such as I - for academics - it might be difficult to reduce our levels of criticality for any extended periods of time. Yet, I understand why it's important to give precedence to Franklism. You have given me much to think about, Ernest.

Ernest

Good. I'm glad.

Noble

I especially like how you have somehow derived a sort of ethical truth from the Pernicious Paradox.

Ernest

Yeah. Me too. It kind of gives you hope, doesn't it?

Noble

Yes. In a way, I suppose it does.

I wonder whether there are more truths that could be derived. The prospect that we might be able to codify derivative atheistic truths into a new fictive morality for philosophical atheists is a truly fascinating idea.

Ernest

Erm. Well, is that really necessary?

Noble

Why wouldn't it be?

Ernest

Well, in a way, you discovered the Pernicious Paradox through being too philosophical. Your search for 'the truth' lead you to Nihilism's dark conclusion.

Now you have a chance to escape it, to find meaning. All you have to do is believe in morality. *Give credence to your conscience* and follow it. That's all you need to do. Nothing more.

Noble

Er--

Ernest

Yesterday you taught me a lot, but if today's conversation has taught us anything it's that you ought to let go of your intellectualism, just a little bit. Or at the very least focus yourself on something other than ethics and morality. We've both been found guilty of putting truth on a pedestal. I think that now it's time for us both to bring it down.

Noble

Yes, but--

Ernest

Is it not now obvious that you'll never find salvation unless you employ a little faith in your conscience? And, I'll say it again: you taught me that, Noble.

Noble

Faith?

Ernest

Yes. Faith.

*   *   *

Ernest and Noble sat together in that ancient pub for a few minutes longer winding down their conversation and finishing off their drinks, under an implied yet mutual understanding that neither of them had won or lost their debate, but also that neither of them really cared about winning or losing anyway. What mattered most to each of them was that the other had managed to evade experiencing the absurd grip of the Pernicious Paradox. As they emerged from Ye Olde Cheshire Cheese Inn onto the wet and shimmering glow of London's moonlit streets, Ernest and Noble equally experienced a moment of transient joy, brought about by a renewed sense of hope, reaffirming for them both the notion that, however unlikely it might seem, meaning can be found in suffering.

As he sought his way home to his bed, where that night he soundly slept, Ernest wondered whether Noble was truly convinced, understanding that academic philosophers are often prone to over-think and under-feel. Yet, he believed that he had successfully planted a seed which - from the impression he got from the look of Noble's improved, albeit damp, demeanour - had begun to sprout before the evening was up. He acknowledged that he had no control over the fate of that flower, yet hoped that Noble now had the will to cherish and feed it himself, and to insist on its beauty rather than to scrutinise it.

Even in the awareness that he'd not fully divulged to Ernest the true extent of his thoughts, Noble now held his student in the highest esteem. When they'd met the day before he'd witnessed the aftermath of a malicious and myopic verbal attack on religion by an ardent and belligerent absolutist, who understood nothing of the importance of meaning. That being so, today it became clear that that absolutism had now absolutely dissolved into a potent and authentic earnestness which was marvellous and contagious and, in many respects, enviable. He wasn't entirely sure in his mind whether he agreed with Ernest's conclusion, that nihilists such as himself should give more credence to their consciences, but in his heart he felt that he was right. For, for the first time in what felt like eons, when Noble peered within himself, he experienced a sense of hope, as if someone had thrown a rope into an otherwise inescapable and destitute ravine, wherein he'd all but resolved himself to the completeness of his own turmoil. Now, thanks to Ernest, Noble had developed the will to find meaning, the very tool required if one is ever to unearth a life worth living.

Epilogue
Afterwards

For some time before he resigned from his PHD, Noble thought and wrote about the implications of what he and Ernest discussed during those two evenings. He considered how *giving credence to the conscience* might work if, as a principle, it was applied to Kantianism, but it proved to be incompatible with Kant's Categorical Imperative. He then attempted to work it into a Teleological theory but found it to be impracticable. He also explored Virtue Ethics, but found himself running in circles evaluating whether *giving credence to the conscience* truly constituted, or even reflected, virtue. Needless to say, Noble thoroughly explored these philosophies and many more but never found a way to make Ernest's idea consistent with any of them.

Whilst this considerably perturbed him at first, he eventually came to the conclusion that Ernest was correct when he said that, if any student of ethics were to rationalise and investigate their own moral convictions, then they would most definitely discover flaws and inconsistencies within them. He resolved, again, just as Ernest had pushed him to concede before but he believed it more completely this time, that *it's important to believe in the value of meaning more than in the value of truth.* And just moments after rediscovering this idea, upon truly and fully comprehending the weight of it in his heart, he drafted and sent in his resignation.

Nowadays Noble works as a refugee support worker, a career path that was inspired by the morals he discovered in the time following his departure from academia. He realised - or rather his conscience told him, upon its full liberation - that everyone must be equal; and thus everyone is equally deserving of a good life. Furthermore, he came to believe that environmentalism was of paramount importance, because it attempted to preserve and strengthen the environments within which everyone's and everything's life-support-system, Planet Earth, can cultivate and create the treasures which ultimately sustain and serve meaning to life. And enabling others to find meaning gave Noble a newly found purpose.

Noble was correct when he said that Ernest would be successful in whatever he did after university, because being awarded a lower second-class honours for his degree didn't bother Ernest, and that in itself was a success. Anyway, Ernest knew he'd probably have to sacrifice his grades when he discovered his calling in life, and he was fine with that. Plus, a degree in itself - the award - like everything else, is only *instrumentally* valuable, he thought; and, in terms of instrumental value, he had learned many things which had lead him to find his calling, his meaning.

A few months after Ernest's and Noble's deep, dark and doomful discussion, reacting to what he consequently saw as his own spiritual ineffability, Ernest went back to the chapel in the Strand Campus with a newly found curiosity for religion. For a while this became a regular fixture in Ernest's life. Often between classes he would take a moment to sit in the quiet of the chapel, to catch up with himself, to appreciate the architecture and acoustics and occasionally to converse with Father Chance about philosophy and, sometimes, even religion.

Before long Ernest and Father Chance found themselves once again exploring the role of Jesus and about the meaning of life according to him. This time Ernest listened, making no attempts to contradict Father Chance's beliefs. Still completely unconvinced by religion and the idea that one must devote their entire life to an unseeable, intangible being in order to receive spiritual salvation, he was surprised to discover that Jesus - as a man, not a god - was a rather likeable character. Ernest knew unconditionally that he could never commit himself to religion. As much as he was no longer an absolutist, he was certain of that. But from that day forward he regularly found himself questioning whether his actions were compatible with Jesus's; whether his life and actions might be approved by someone such as him, regardless of whether or not he existed in the form that Christianity professes that he did.

Consequently, he spent many of his remaining days as a student volunteering at various homeless shelters around London, and continues doing so to this day. Through showing to Noble that it is prudent to try to enable oneself to find meaning, Ernest had decided that it must therefore be *right* to try to enable others to find meaning also. And there is meaning in *trying*, he thought, whether or not we triumph in doing so.

END

Printed in Great Britain
by Amazon